The Spindrift Anthology

To my grand daughter
Laura
with much love,
Grandma
11/00

The Tarpon Springs Writers Group

Spindrift Productions
Palm Harbor, Florida

Cover Design by
Robyn Hillary

Story Illustrations by
Robert Dockery

Library of Congress Catalog Card Number: 00 133466
ISBN # 0-9702408-0-5
First Printing, 2000

 For further information or to reach an author, please contact: Spindrift Productions, 305 Bay Street, Palm Harbor, Florida 34683.

Table of Contents

Table of Contents (cont.)

Children's Stories:

Foreward

Writing is a lonely business. Other creative artists can display their work on a wall, play it on a piano, watch it grow, or build it. Writers work alone, staring at their typewriters or PC's and receiving little feedback.

To assuage this loneliness, give mutual understanding, and encourage excellence, creative writing groups are founded. For more than a dozen years, the Tarpon Springs Writers Group has met at 10 a.m. every Friday in a city library room to read and critique original prose writing intended for publication. There are no dues and no elected officers; all subjects and all genre are acceptable.

Membership in the group includes writers from all fields. We have a mystery writer who has published more than 28 books in her career; a novelist whose first book has been accepted by St. Martin's Press; a veteran of the publishing industry; journalists collaborating to sell articles to police magazines; an historic novelist; writers of children's fiction; a *Reader's Digest* contributor; and many more.

At a typical session, writers read to the group short stories, chapters from novels, articles, query letters or other material intended for publication. Selections take approximately twenty minutes to read. Then each member of the group takes a turn giving a critique of the material. Critiques focus on technical mistakes, unclear passages, mistakes in grammar and usage, narrative strength, point of view, time and place, plot and character development, and the potential for publication. Writers are advised not to become sensitive or defensive because all criticism is intended as a positive effort. We emphasize respect and professionalism.

Well aware that the book and periodical market in the United States is highly competitive, rigorous in its standards, and difficult to enter, the Tarpon Springs writers are committed to producing excellence. This sample of our writing is our way of displaying what we can offer the reading public.

We would like to thank the Tarpon Springs Library for its support of our efforts and for providing us with a meeting facility. It is appropriate that we work in its precincts because the library is the storehouse of the creativity we strive to emulate.

In My Craft or Sullen Art

In my craft or sullen art
Exercised in the still night
When only the moon rages
And the lovers lie abed
With all their griefs in their arms,
I labour by singing light
Not for ambition or bread
Or the strut and trade of charms
On the ivory stages
But for the common wages
Of their most secret heart.

Not for the proud man apart
From the raging moon I write
On these spindrift pages
Nor for the towering dead
With their nightingales and psalms
But for the lovers, their arms
Round the griefs of the ages,
Who pay no praise or wages
Nor heed my craft or art.

— *Dylan Thomas (1946)*

The Spindrift Anthology

Deepwater Doug and Filthyfoot

by Howard Jones

We needed a captain and a boat. Our favorite charter boat had burned and sunk about forty miles southeast of Montauk. We weren't aboard that day. Fortunately nobody was hurt, but Captain Stanger's boat went to the bottom, together with his net worth.

Jim heard about it and tried to call him, but couldn't find him. He was gone from the Star Island Marina and the Montauk charter fishing community. The people at the Marina said they thought he would wait out the season to let the publicity blow away.

Jim called Brandon, the boss bartender at the Neptune, a favorite hangout for the Montauk captains.

"We need a boat, Brandon, for either August 8th or 9th, with a captain who can find us some fish. We've got some big-time customers who want to go fishing."

"What kind of fish you looking for, Jim?"

"We aren't going to be fussy. We just need to show these guys some action. We'd love to hook into some giant tuna, or a marlin or a sail, but we'd settle for a couple of big sharks, maybe even a Mako."

"Let me think," Brandon said. "Give me a minute." The phone was silent for twenty seconds.

"Jim, there's a captain comes in here name of Doug Rankin. He's got a 46-foot Bertram named Susan II. Likes to run out deep. The guys call him Deepwater Doug. I think he'd get you some fish."

"Sounds like our guy, Brandon. You have his phone number?"

"Call me tomorrow, Jim. I should have it"

Jim got the number from Brandon the next evening and called Captain Doug Rankin. They had a good discussion about the fishing out of Montauk harbor, what they might expect to catch. They decided that because it would be a one-day trip they wouldn't go the ninety miles to the deep water at the "canyon" where the ocean floor dropped thousands of feet and the deep blue water of the gulf stream swept up from the Caribbean, bringing with it giant marlin and big-eye tuna.

Instead they would stay within forty or fifty miles and fish for sailfish, shark and whatever else struck their lures. They agreed on August 8th.

After lunch on August 7th, Jim, Robin and I left their marketing company on Park Avenue South, picked up Roger and Mike at the Reader's Digest office, then battled the Long

Island traffic out Highway 495, across on 46 to 27, and out through the Hamptons. We stopped near Shinnecock Harbor for a couple of quick drinks to break up the trip, then on to the tip of the South Fork of Long Island, where we checked into the Sandbar Motel.

At 5 o'clock the next morning we were breakfasting with dozens of sleepy fishermen, captains and mates at Salivar's. Before 6:00 we were inquiring about the Susan II. She was dark when we found her. No lights and activity such as there was around the other boats getting ready for the day's fishing. She looked to be a little old but in pretty good condition, if rather plainly and sparsely equipped.

We waited on the dock for ten minutes, then Jim suggested we go aboard. We settled down on the aft deck to wait. Jim went forward through the cabin, past the controls, toward the bunks and the head. On the port bunk, thrust back toward the entrance to the bunk area, Jim saw two filthy feet with ragged, curving toenails, protruding from tattered trousers. His astonished gaze traveled upwards along greasy dungarees and a dirty blue shirt to a face and head covered with scraggly, tangled hair. The apparition was sodden with dirt, blood, and fish scales.

Jim quickly withdrew and motioned Robin and me to silently follow him forward. We peered open-mouthed at the creature on the bunk.

Back on deck Robin said, "I've heard of Bigfoot the Sasquatch. I believe we've found Filthyfoot of Montauk."

When they looked in again the bag of rags was stirring. Just then the dock lights at the stern went on, and there was Captain Doug, with a kraft paper bag under his arm.

"Morning, gentlemen," he said with a forced smile. He climbed aboard, tossed his paper bag into the cabin, and stiffly met each of the five members of his fishing party. He was medium stature, about 60, a thin studious face with glasses, not the picture of the usual Montauk captain.

At that point the ragged, man-beast emerged from the cabin, yawning and scratching himself. Captain Doug glanced at him, then turned back to the fishermen gathered in the stern. "That is Robert, your mate. Go get the bait, Robert."

Still barefoot, Robert climbed up on the dock and disappeared toward the supply store.

"You fellas got your supplies? — food, booze, soft drinks? It's a long day out there."

"We're all set Captain. Where do you want us to stow the stuff?" I asked.

"There's a big cooler just inside the cabin door. If one of you will get some ice, I'll fire up the engines and we'll get ready to go."

"I'll get the ice," Robin volunteered, and took off toward the Marina store.

The Captain flipped open the hatch and leaned down with a flashlight to inspect the two big diesels. I took Jim's arm and walked him to the stern.

"Deepwater Doug and Filthyfoot," I said. "Might be an interesting day. Any second thoughts?"

"It's kinda crazy, but let's go with it. We could have some extra fun." Jim broke an impish grin, and turned to talk with the guests.

Filthyfoot returned with several plastic bags of chum and some frozen bait fish, at about the same time Robin brought the ice. Captain Doug had started both engines, now idling smoothly. Filthyfoot cast off the tie-ups. Doug eased her out of the marina into the harbor, out past Grossman's sprawling restaurant, through the opening in the breakwater and into the Atlantic.

He let her run at mid-RPMs as we cruised along the beach and campground, past the lighthouse. When we nosed into the first big rollers, Doug moved the throttles up to full cruising RPMs.

The diesels had the Bertram up and flying, driving her out at 20-plus knots toward the deep water. Filthyfoot took the wheel in the cabin while Captain Doug climbed up to the flying bridge where he had a better view of the ocean, and again took control .

Robin and Jim went into the cabin and broke out the vodka and grapefruit juice, building an early morning eye-opener for the fishermen, then we all settled down in the cabin for the rough two-and a-half hour ride to the fishing area.

Filthyfoot dragged his three bags of aged fish to the port side aft, began to cut them into small pieces and toss them into a dented bucket.

Watching from the cabin with the others, Jim said, "I think the other captains buy their chum already cut up and frozen in neat, net bags."

"Possibly our captain is a bit penurious," Roger mused.

"He probably doesn't pay Filthyfoot anything, just a place to sleep, and all the chum he can eat," Robin said.

"It could be the cheapest chum out of Montauk, but it may be the best. It sure is strong!" He held his nose as the reek of the rotten fish whipped back toward the cabin.

In the next hour, Filthyfoot filled three buckets with chopped, stinking, fish, lashed them to the transom, washed and mopped the deck and drained it all out the scuppers. Then he set up the fighting chair and began to bring out the heavy, expensive fishing gear — two strong rods with big Penn reels fitted into the sockets on each side of the boat, each with a different artificial lure. He hooked the lures to the leaders, ready to throw overboard when we slowed down to trolling speed.

At about 9 o'clock Captain Doug brought down the RPMs and the Bertram settled lower in the water, but kept driving through the four foot waves. Doug was standing on the bridge now, gazing around at the horizon. I climbed up to join him.

"Looking for birds. Birds usually mean fish in the area,"

Doug said. "Maybe even see a fin. Keep a sharp lookout. There could be some action around here."

In the next half-hour we saw two Basking sharks, not game fish, but nothing else. Finally Doug cut the motors and motioned to Filthyfoot to set out the outriggers and run out the baits. Soon we were dragging several different lures. Doug set the controls to a rapid trolling speed and started to curve her around in a big half-mile circle, over water where he'd had some success in the past.

We were ten minutes into the run when I grabbed Doug's shoulder and pointed over the port quarter.

"Fin," I said, excitement making my voice rise in spite of my effort to stay cool.

Doug followed my gaze and pointing arm.

"Got him!" Doug said. "Big sailfish, by God. He's running away from our course; we've got to swing over and cut across his nose with our baits."

He swung the boat to the left and hit the throttles, causing the four fishermen and Filthyfoot to come alive, jump up and look up at the bridge.

"Got a fin out there! We're going to take the baits across in front of him," I called down. "Who is first in the chair, just in case he hits one of them?"

"Mike's turn. We'll get him ready. You stay up there and help the Captain keep an eye on that fish," Robin said.

"There he is again, see the fin?" I was pointing at 8 o'clock off the port side."

"Got him! Got him! I see him!" Jim yelled. He grabbed the guests and turned them toward the sail-like fin slicing along the surface in a straight line.

"What is it?" Robin called up to the bridge.

"Captain says its a sailfish, big one."

"Whooee, let's get him," Robin whooped.

Just then the sail disappeared.

"He's gone," Jim said.

"Maybe not. He's around here somewhere," Robin said, watching the gray waves intently.

Doug swung the boat around to the port to try to run directly ahead of the path of the fish. Nothing happened. Two minutes passed.

"Goddam, Goddam, we missed him," Doug roared from the bridge.

We ran another two minutes on the same course, then the line on the starboard outrigger snapped loose with a sharp crack. Five seconds later the reel on a rod in the starboard rail started to sing.

"Got him! Got him!," Robin shouted

"Not yet, we haven't."

Filthyfoot had moved to the rod with the spinning, singing reel.

"Let him eat it. Let him have it. Don't set it yet," Doug was calling directions from the bridge.

Filthyfoot had the rod, carrying it along the transom toward the chair, keeping the tip pointed to where he thought the fish was.

"All right, set it! Set it!" Doug shouted.

Filthyfoot set up the drag and heaved back on the rod.

"Set it again. Set it hard!"

Filthyfoot, intently watching the line and concentrating on the fish, took another step toward the fighting chair to hand the rod to the fisherman after another hard set of the hook. Some blood and slime from the chum buckets had flowed along the deck beneath his feet.

When he heaved back on the rod his bare feet lost all traction and he fell heavily backward on the deck. The rod crashed against the transom, loosening the hook in the fish's mouth. Robin grabbed the rod to keep it from going overboard. He hauled back on the rod, but there was no resistance.

"Reel, reel! He may be running toward us!" Doug shouted.

Robin reeled crazily, but the line remained slack.

"Reel," Doug shouted. "He could still be on there."

Robin kept reeling until the leader showed.

"He's gone. Long gone," Jim said.

Their concentration swung from the lost fish to Filthyfoot, who was still motionless on the deck.

"My gosh, he's unconscious," Roger exclaimed. "He's out. Doesn't seem to be breathing. He must have really smashed his head on the deck."

Robin quickly knelt by the prone figure. He put his ear near the mouth, then his finger on the pulse in the neck. "There's no pulse, and he doesn't seem to be breathing. I'll start the CPR. He felt around Filthyfoot's mouth with his index finger to make sure the passage was clear, laid three fingers on the man's chest to find the spot near his sternum, then started the rhythmic push, push, push, fifteen times, and wait. He looked up at Jim.

"I think he needs mouth-to-mouth," he said. Jim's jaw dropped slightly as he stared at Robin, then at the slack, scruffy mouth. A few seconds passed

"You going to do it?" I asked.

Jim walked over to the rail, breathed deeply, and looked out across the gray Atlantic. He turned back and slowly shook his head.

"No," he said.

Filthyfoot broke the impasse by groaning, rolling his head side-to-side and gasping a deep, gurgling breath.

Robin stopped his ministrations, got to his feet, and with Roger's help, got Filthyfoot upright.

Doug had been watching impassively from the bridge. "He'll be OK," he said. "He's tough as those sharks out there."

"Let's start chumming," he called down to his mate, who was staggering across the deck shaking his head to clear it.

Suddenly it was silent. Doug had cut the engines and the Bertram began its mid-day drift. Filthyfoot took his position in the starboard aft corner, and began to chuck pieces of chum overboard. They would slowly sink toward the ocean floor, and trail out in a long bloody necklace. Along the surface would be a lengthening oil slick.

Eventually, a shark or another fish would cross the string of rotten fish or the oily surface smear, and follow it to the boat. Others would follow. Sharks have a super sensory affinity for bloody, rotten fish.

The Susan II rocked lazily in the swells. The mid-morning sun burned through the overcast and the group, sprawled about the deck and cabin, began to peel off garments. Jim mixed drinks for the fishermen, finishing just as Captain Doug came down from the flying bridge.

"Would you like a drink, Captain?" Jim asked

Doug hesitated a moment. "Yeah. Don't mind if I do. Thanks."

"What'll it be?"

"Just some vodka over ice would be fine," Doug replied.

Jim put a handful of ice cubes in a glass and filled it more than half full with vodka. Doug took a long drink from the glass, swallowing several times, and moved to the controls at the front of the cabin. Robin looked at Jim and raised his eyebrows slightly.

There were a few creaks and rattles as the boat rocked and drifted, and the occasional "plop" as Filthyfoot spooned some more chum over the side. Doug finished the half-glass of vodka and emerged from the cabin with a full-rigged rod and reel. The reel and the space around it presented a massive tangle of nylon fishing line.

"I had some real tenderfeet out yesterday," Doug explained to Robin, who had moved over to see what he was doing. "I'm going to untangle this thing. I've got many dollars worth of line wrapped up here."

Doug stood at the port rail and worked at the line while the others began to watch for fins. Jim also moved over to watch Doug. "Want another little bump of vodka, Captain, to make that less frustrating?"

"Yeah, that's a good idea," Doug turned and grinned at Jim, the first sign of levity from the Captain.

Jim brought another half-glass. Doug took a deep draft from the glass and set it on the rail. A few minutes later Robin took Jim by the arm and walked him toward the front of the cabin.

"I think we've been generous enough with the Captain. We don't know his capacity and tolerance, and we're a long way out on this ocean," he said.

Jim grinned. "I agree. Just wanted to bring down the barriers and have a friendly trip.

The turn in the chair was changed every half-hour. Roger was now in the chair.

Just after noon Jim and Robin began to make up some sandwiches from the groceries in the cooler. Doug left his tangled line carefully braced against the rail and wandered in. "Any of that vodka left?"

After a brief hesitation Jim said, "Sure, Captain. Let me rinse your glass and pour you a fresh one."

Robin shook his head behind Doug's back and stepped out on the deck to help watch for some fishing action. Roger, lounging in the fishing chair, suddenly came to life. "I see something! What is that? Is that a fish?"

"Fin! Fin! Shark! We've got a fish!" Robin shouted.

Filthyfoot was up instantly, checking the drags on the reels. Jim looked at the Captain, still working on the tangled line by the rail.

"Shouldn't we be moving Captain? Get the boat moving? What if we get a strike? Shouldn't we be ready to move with the fish?"

"No, just hold tight. Stay with the chum line. You don't have a fish on yet," Doug replied.

" There's another fin, and there's another!" Mike sang out.

"Yeaow! We got sharks. Here we go!" Robin whooped.

The rod in the aft port corner dipped. Robin jumped to grab it.

"Don't hit him yet. Let him eat it," Jim barked.

Ten seconds. The rod dipped again, bending sharply, then the reel started its high-pitched buzz.

"Hit him, Robin. Hit him!"

Filthyfoot had stepped up to do his duty as mate and deliver the jumping rod to the fisherman in the fighting chair, but Jim waved him away. Robin had muscled the rod out of its seat in the rail and carried it over to Roger in the fighting chair. He jammed it into the gimbal between Roger's knees, handed him the rod, grunting with the effort of holding it against the fish, and buckled it to the harness around Roger's shoulders.

"OK, fight him baby. You got a few hundred pounds of shark on there," Robin said.

Roger grasped the rod with both hands and began to pull against the fish. Robin was firing instructions to him about how to pump the rod and gain line, and how to handle the drag so he wouldn't break the line or get pulled over the transom into the ocean. Jim was behind Roger, keeping the swivel chair pointed toward the fish so the line and rod pulled straight. I scurried up the ladder to the flying bridge to watch the action and con the boat if required. Filthyfoot and Mike were bringing in the other lines, and Doug continued to untangle the line at the port rail.

The shark was going down, down, taking hundreds of yards of line.

Robin was helping Roger regulate the drag on the reel, to

gradually slow the monster, and start to tire him.

Roger was beginning to grunt with the exertion of holding the straining, jumping rod, trying to get the tip up and reel in some line.

Filthyfoot finished bringing in the other lines, and slowly climbed the ladder to relieve me at the controls. The diesels were still idling.

"Should we keep chumming?" Jim asked Doug.

"Yeah, throw some over. If we lose this one we'll keep the others around."

Jim held his nose and scooped some of the stinking mess over the side.

For awhile it appeared that Roger was moving the fish. He was able to gain a little line by pulling up the tip of the rod, then reeling as he dropped it toward the water. Then the fish stopped, as if it was anchored to the bottom. Roger was beginning to tire, his face pouring sweat, his body soaked.

"Maybe we should back the boat down on him a little and gain some line," Robin suggested to the Captain.

Doug looked up briefly from his tangled line and shouted up to the bridge, "Back her down a little."

Filthyfoot moved over to the controls. The throaty rumble started up from the diesels. Robin was waving for him to back the boat toward the fish. Filthyfoot seemed to be having trouble getting it into reverse.

Finally, with a grinding thump he got it. Filthyfoot pushed the throttles forward and suddenly they were rapidly backing toward the fish, much faster than Roger could reel in the line.

"Stop! Stop!" Robin was screaming. "You'll back over the line."

Filthyfoot seemed confused. The boat continued to back up rapidly, building up a big surge of water behind the transom.

Robin, quiet Robin, his face turning purple, was dancing a wild jig by the fighting chair, shaking his fist at the frenzied

Filthyfoot who was desperately trying to stop the boat.

Robin was screaming an incredible and magnificent string of obscenities and invective at the bridge. It went on and on, searing across the foggy Atlantic, warming the jet stream, and eventually changing the climate for several days in Denmark and Normandy.

The tip of the rod bent down sharply, then snapped upright. The line hung limp as the props caught it, tangled and cut it. Roger lunged back in the chair and the fish was free.

Robin charged to the foot of the ladder, screaming at Filthyfoot, although hoarseness was beginning to dim the decibels. Jim and I were laughing so hard we were holding on to each other to keep upright.

Mike wasn't quite sure what was happening. Doug calmly climbed the ladder to the bridge, pushed Filthyfoot aside, disengaged the clutches and returned the engines to idle.

Robin was still seething. "What the hell goes on here? Doesn't anybody know how to fish? Who's running this goddam boat?"

Doug looked down at him with hurt and disdain. "No need to swear at us," he said.

The fishermen gathered in the cabin to mix drinks and whisper to each other in wonder. Outside, a cowering Filthyfoot was re-rigging the boat for further shark hunting. While they were finishing the drinks in the cabin, Captain Doug brought in the fishing rig he had been working on.

"Untangled it. Saved fifty dollars worth of line," he said, as he fitted it into the rack in the roof of the cabin.

He returned to the rail, got his empty glass and re-entered the cabin.

"Any of that vodka left?" he asked.

Nobody moved or spoke. Finally Jim said, "Sure Captain." He put a handful of ice cubes into the glass and filled it two-thirds full of vodka.

Doug went out, and stood surveying the set-up and the sea.

Robin gave Jim a quizzical look.

"He's the Captain, and he gave me an order," Jim said defensively.

"This is some circus," Robin said, shaking his head.

Filthyfoot was chumming, the boat was again rolling slowly in the swells, when Doug said sharply, "Get somebody in the chair. We've got sharks again."

It was Jim's turn. He climbed into the chair and buckled in. The rod on his left jumped, and the reel began to buzz as the line ran out against the drag.

"Got one on," Robin shouted, and muscled the rod up to Jim.

With an experienced fisherman in the chair, the fight went better.

Jim held the fish from going deep, and slowly started to haul him in. In less than fifteen minutes they saw the leader, then the dark shape in the water. When the shark saw the boat and the fishermen gesturing and moving about, it went crazy, thrashing and shaking its head to get free. Jim was pulling with all his strength, losing line.

Captain Doug had gone to the cabin and returned waving a .38 six-shooter pistol. He elbowed up to the rail and began shooting at the big, Blue Shark.

The shark suddenly made a run to the side. Robin swung the chair so the rod and line would be running straight to the fish. The swing scrambled the onlookers along the rear transom, and threw off Doug's aim. A shot went zinging off the rail. He ducked around to get to the rail close to the fish, waving the pistol.

Robin exploded. "Jesus Christ, Captain. Put the pistol away. You're going to kill somebody. Man, this is too hairy for me."

Doug emptied the pistol at the shark, then turned to Robin.

"This is my boat, and I am the captain. Don't tell me when

to use my pistol." He stalked to the cabin and tossed the pistol into a box near the wheel. He found his glass, returned again to the cabin, and without asking, poured himself three-quarters of a glass of vodka, no ice.

Doug had actually hit the shark a few times. The water was bloody. Jim hauled it in close enough so Robin could grab the leader and pull the fish up to the boat. The shark had swallowed the lure, so he cut the leader just ahead of the shark's nose. The fish began to sink, dead in the water. His friends would tear him to pieces and devour him before he hit the bottom 300 feet below.

The chum and the blood in the water kept the sharks in the area. It was Robin's turn in the chair. In ten minutes the line snapped off the starboard outrigger, and we had another shark on. I gave the bent-over rod to Robin, who buckled and snapped himself in for the fight.

Robin let it have line for awhile, then slowly tightened the drag and stopped the line from running out. Then the fight began, — gain some line, then lose some to the shark against the drag. Doug sat up on the flying bridge, watching with wavering interest.

Twenty minutes later Robin had the fish hauled up near the boat.

Captain Doug had come down and poured himself another three-fourths glass of vodka, and climbed shakily back up to the bridge.

Robin was groaning with the strain as he hauled back on the rod again and again. "I'll bring it close, and you try to get a good picture of it alive in the water," he gasped.

I had the waterproof camera out, shooting the thrashing, frantic fish, working around the chair and the boat trying to get a perfect angle.

Jim spoke to Filthyfoot, "I'll try to gaff him and bring him in close, then you club him hard and we'll try to get your lure back. I hope he isn't too green. I could lose the gaff and maybe my arm."

Filthyfoot took the club and went to the other side of the chair.

Robin brought the fish in close in a violent, thrashing sweep, and Jim caught it behind the gill with the gaff.

"Hit him," he shouted at Filthyfoot.

The mate took a powerful swing and missed. Both he and Jim nearly went over the transom into the water with the fish. Filthyfoot recovered, ran to the other side of the chair, took another big swing and connected. The shark went quiet. Mike quickly grabbed the gaff handle to help Jim, and together they pulled the fish partly out of the water. Filthyfoot poked at the lure in the shark's mouth with his club, and it popped loose. Mike let go of his hold on the gaff, then Jim with a quick push freed the gaff, and the fish slipped away.

They stood gasping, looking at each other, shaking their heads about the crazy, wild exertion they had been through. Jim looked up at the bridge where Captain Doug had been silently, boozily watching the fight.

Jim looked away, and shook his head in disgust.

They drifted for another hour, with me then Mike in the chair, but no fish struck. Captain Doug seemed to be asleep with his eyes open.

Jim and Robin had a quick conference in the cabin.

"I think he is going to pass out. It's getting choppy and a little late. Let's head back," Robin said. Jim agreed.

They stepped out on deck. "Let's go in, Captain. That's enough action for today," Robin called up to the bridge.

"Yeah, right. Good idea," Doug mumbled.

"Bring 'em in Robert, let's go," he shouted to the mate.

Filthyfoot, with help from Robin and me, reeled in the baits, and stowed the rods in the cabin. Doug put it in gear, and began to run up the RPMs

"He going in the right direction?" Jim asked Robin.

They looked around them at the horizon. It had turned cloudy and gray, no sun, no shadows. They were more than fifty miles out of Montauk.

"I wonder if he can see the compass," Robin said.

Jim climbed the ladder to the bridge. "Want me to take her for awhile, Captain?" he offered.

Doug hesitated, fumbling with wheel and throttles. "Yeah, good idea. Think I'll go down for a little nap."

He worked his way shakily down the ladder. Three steps above the deck his legs and grip seemed to give out at the same time, and he started a teetering fall. Before he hit the deck Filthyfoot was there, caught him in his arms, heaved him up to a full carrying position, staggered forward and gently laid him on a bunk. Doug was out cold.

Filthyfoot looked down at the lightly breathing captain, shook his head, then climbed up to the bridge and stood next to Jim.

"That was a great save. We're proud of you," Jim said. "Think we can find Montauk?"

Filthyfoot nodded and pointed to a position on the compass. Jim swung the Bertram to that heading, and revved it up to cruising speed.

"Here we go. It's Montauk, Martha's Vineyard or Ireland, damned if I know," Jim called to the rest of us on deck.

He held the boat on course for nearly an hour, seeing nothing in the haze but the gray waves rushing past. Jim called me to the bridge.

"Help me watch forward. We don't want to run into a shoreline, or another boat, or a ship."

We could see only about 200 yards ahead in the gray weather. For another forty minutes we stared into the haze.

"Boat! Boat!" I sang out.

Angling in toward our course was another fishing boat.

"Thank God. We can follow him in. Hope he is going to Montauk."

"Let's try to get him on the radio," Jim said.

I tried, but I couldn't make contact.

Forty-five minutes later the Montauk light showed on the port quarter, and we knew for sure where we were. We ran in along the beach to the harbor entrance

When Jim cut the throttle to turn inside the breakwater Captain Doug stirred, stretched, yawned, and climbed the ladder to the bridge.

"Thanks for your help, I'll take her in," he said softly.

Jim relinquished the wheel and the throttles, staring incredulously at the composed, quiet man. Deepwater Doug skillfully brought her into the marina, and carefully backed her into the narrow slip. With barely a bump the big boat snuggled against the planks.

The fishermen on Susan II stood and stretched, and began to toss their gear up to the dock. From the cabin Captain Doug brought out a neatly rendered bill.

"Enjoyed the trip, gentlemen. Hope we will do it again soon," he said.

"It was an extraordinary trip, Captain," Jim said as he handed him the check.

Robin and I turned away, shoulders shaking

Filthyfoot was hosing down the deck, bloody water sloshing across his claw-tipped, bare feet.

Howard Jones left rural South Dakota for the U.S. Air Force, then to the University of Minnesota School of Journalism. He worked in advertising and magazine publishing in the frozen Northland until recently moving to Florida, to thaw out in the sunshine and write stories.

Grampa's Lessons

by E. True

Hoss

The little horse was called "Hoss"; just Hoss. When there were two other big horses and a yoke of oxen in the barn, names were needed, but the big horses and oxen were gone. Grampa couldn't do the heavy hard work he used do. ... "Fore I come t'close 't eighty years old" he said.

He'd sold off his yokes of oxen and team of big work horses. He kept the little horse to pull the "Democrat buggy" to do errands or to visit elderly friends. Grampa never accepted the "Infernal" Combustion Engine. "I'm too old for these new fangled things."

My most impressive happening at that time was going to the salt marsh with Grandpa when I was four years old.

Grampa was getting things ready to go haying. He had done most of the chores, gone over the wagon and tools, sharpened the sickle bars and scythe blades. Everything was in order but for Hoss. He needed new shoes.

The next morning before he went to work, Pa put me on Hoss and said, "If you can't see a train, you can go cross the railroad tracks to the big road. There you turn right. The Blacksmiths is just beyond the Jackman house. You can't miss it - it's under the big Elm tree 'bout a mile after you get to the big road."

I took the reins, gave them a shake, and said, "Gidiyup." Hoss went up the road to the end of the barn. Then, he knew he shouldn't go any further with just a kid. He ignored me, turned around and went back into the farm yard.

Pa took the halter, led Hoss up the road past the barn and gave him a hard slap on the flank and said, "Git up there." Hoss kept going.

I worried all the way. Did Hoss know where we were going? Which house was the Jackman House? — I didn't know there were so many houses — or Elm trees! The blacksmith met me on the road.

At the Blacksmith's shop I watched as the Smithy did things to Hoss' hoofs. He tried a couple of horse shoes for size, explained his forge to me and how he "cleaned" the hoofs and shaped the shoes on the anvil. After he finished work on Hoss' hoofs, he walked Hoss about a bit to see how he walked, then tied him to a hitching post in the shade of the big tree.

While we waited for Pa to come the Smithy made a ring from a horseshoe nail for my finger. He heated it red hot, holding it in some smaller pliers, then hit it lightly with a small hammer and swished it about in the big water tank. I was afraid it would burn, but it was just warm.

Pa came along in his Model "T" Ford and talked with the Smithy a few moments; then he put me on Hoss and told me to "Head for home, I'll catch up to you."

The Salt Marsh

The morning of going to the marsh I remember well. I was so disappointed when my Grandma said, "He is too young to go to the marsh! He doesn't even go to school until this fall." Grampa won that debate by saying, "I need him, I can't go to the salt marsh all alone. If I need help he can go and get it for me."

What's salt marsh? .... "Well, remember when we went to the beach to swim in the ocean last summer? You asked about why nothing was growing on those nice great big flat fields between the woods and the ocean. The grass that grows there will not grow well any place but where the ocean tides keep the ground wet with ocean water. Not much other than that grass can grow there because ocean water is very salty."

In the morning as I ate my oatmeal, Mom made up my lunch and Grampa harnessed Hoss. I helped when I got out there by hooking the horse to the wagon and helped Grampa get the gear box and tools on the wagon. After Grampa had checked my hook up, and put a couple of grain bags half full of hay for cushions on the tool box, I waved good bye to Mom and we left.

At the edge of the salt marsh I helped Grampa get the bog shoes out of the gear box and held Hoss' bridle while he strapped them on Hoss' hooves.

Bog shoes? "They are a lot like snow shoes are for a man who has to walk in deep snow. Only Hoss' bog shoes were made of square hard wood strips with flat iron reinforcing bars on the corners, and on the bottom, for the horse to stand on. They are strapped to the horse's hooves with strong leather straps. It takes a smart horse to learn to walk with them because they are wider than his hooves. But they do let a horse walk on the marsh without sinking through the sod that lies on top of the soft muck underneath."

With the bog shoes firmly strapped in place we went out on the marsh. I went to work raking up the hay that had been cut the day before. While I raked that wet grass into bunches, Grampa made small haycocks of the wet grass so the breeze would blow through it and it would dry in the sun.

We finished that and Grampa loaded the dry hay in the wagon while I tramped it down. Everything went well until Pa came after he was through working at his job. He was not as patient as Grandpa, and he hurried the little horse. (This may have caused a bog shoe to loosen and come off one hoof). That hoof broke through the sod; Hoss fell. Of course he struggled trying to get up, but Grampa calmed him quickly and got him to lie still on the ground. Then he had to calm me and convince me that I had to sit on Hoss' head, "just so," to keep him quiet so he wouldn't hurt himself. Pa convinced me quickly with a couple of swats on my rear.

Grandpa and Pa had to unhitch the wagon, and drag it back out of the way. Then they had to dig the sod and muck away from the leg so the horse would be able to stand up again. It was awfully hard to sit just as Grampa had told me to do, so I wouldn't hurt Hoss. They had to dig for a long time to get Hoss' leg free. While they dug I patted Hoss and talked to him. If I looked down between my knees I could see one eye looking questions at me.

Finally Grampa came over to me and said, "You stay right there now; you're doing a good job and we're 'most done." I sat there on the horse's head while Grampa got a spare bog shoe out of the gear box and strapped it on the hoof.

Soon Grampa came back to me again, and said, "We're 'bout all set. Now you get up real slow, so you don't scare Hoss, and move 'way back out of the way." Grampa started talking to Hoss. He took hold of Hoss's bridle with one hand and, when I was out of the way, an ear with the other hand. Then Grampa said to Hoss, "Now up with you Hoss, — up —, up," As Grampa pulled on the bridle, Hoss lunged to his feet. "Easy now, boy - eez - easy boy, good boy" and he patted the horse's neck as Hoss stood trembling, leaning his head against Grampa's chest.

Grampa walked Hoss around a bit and watched to see that he walked all right. Satisfied, Grampa hooked him to the wagon and watched Hoss again to see if the wagon bothered him any. It didn't, so we put the rest of the dry hay on the wagon. Grampa put me on the seat and lead Hoss ashore .... to the higher land that the high tides didn't reach.

There on the high land, while I held Hoss' bridle, Grampa took the bog shoes off Hoss's hoofs and put them in the gear box. He then checked to see that everything was stowed properly. Grampa, climbing up beside me on the seat on the tool box, gave me the reins and said, "Let's go home. I'm tired. You drive."

While Grampa and I were taking care of Hoss and the hay, Pa had filled the hole, and already had cranked up his Model "T" Ford and left for home. I didn't know the way home, but I started Hoss up a path. Hoss knew where to go and he went with a will. He took Grampa and me home safely.

As soon as we finished off-loading the hay and put the wagon away, we took Hoss back to the barn. When we took his harness off, Hoss hurried into his nice safe stall. There I combed him down while Grampa rubbed lineament into the stressed leg. When I finished Grampa told me, "All I do is rub it in like this for a few more minutes. You can go ahead in now."

The Fork Handle

It was at least forty or fifty years later when I realized how important the last big lesson from Grampa was. It has stuck with me for most of these years. It was a simple instruction. "If it's worth doing, do it right."

I was twelve years old when I broke a fork handle as we hurried to get the last of the hay into the barn before a thunder storm hit. I heaved hard on the fork as I'd been told never to do. It broke.

That evening, I had just finished eating, when Grampa came into the dining room and said, “Boy, get your axe. You have a handle to make!”

I wondered all the way down to the grove of small ash trees near the brook, how I could make a good fork handle with an axe. Grampa studied many small, just-past-sapling-size ash, and selected a small tree with few low limbs. He had me cut it down, trim the limbs close to the trunk, peel the bark, cut it to his length mark and put the piece on some rocks that held it under water above the bottom in the brook. I’d received my instructions on the way down to the grove.

I waded back to the bank and as I was finishing getting my socks back on my damp feet I heard, “You did pretty good boy, but you made one mistake. .... What was it?” I thought about it for several minutes before he said, “I told you on the way down here, you always put the “balk” for a tool handle in the stream, butt end up stream. It washes the sap out much better that way.”

He followed this with a gentle, “You don’t listen well, Boy.” I have never forgotten that totally. It still comes back when I know I’ve done a poor job of something.

That summer I spent much time evenings, smoothing and rubbing linseed oil into that handle, curing it to Grampa’s satisfaction. That handle lasted many years.

Grampa taught me much about patience also by example. He was always calm and patient with his animals, often telling me, “Be patient! You’re much smarter than the poor dumb critters.”

Apple Cider

Fall is the season for making apple cider. Autumn in New England is called “Fall,” or “The Fall.” According to Webster, “deciduous” means “to fall, as leaves in autumn.”

Grampa's Lessons

In New England the leaves turn many colors before they fall. Swamp Maple leaves turn scarlet, Sugar Maple's become bright yellow, Birch and Poplar leaves are yellow, Red Oak leaves turn late and are almost maroon. White Oak leaves hang on the tree most of the winter, slowly bleaching to tan. There are many shades of these colors. Each tree has its time and color. Many trees become huge bouquets in the autumn.

I was in the third grade, a bit past eight years old, when I first helped Grampa get the cider made. After school, as usual, I went straight home to do my chores which at that particular time meant picking up the "Drops", the apples that had fallen off the trees in the apple orchard or been dropped during harvest. I worked at that task every day for a week or so.

After school Friday I helped Grampa load the wagon. It took one of us on each end of the bags. The load on the wagon was as big as the little old horse could pull easily on a long haul. It takes a lot of apples to make three barrels of cider.

It was getting dark by the time we got the load to the barn, unhitched the wagon, unharnessed Hoss, and rubbed him down. After putting him in his stall, I gave him his forkful of hay and scoop of oats. Grampa had already given him good fresh bedding. We called it a day. Tomorrow was the big day. We were going to the cider mill.

In the morning Grampa came to get me while I was finishing my breakfast oatmeal. He asked my mother if she had packed my lunch, then checked it and me. He then made a suggestion or two to Mom and said to me, "I'll be getting things ready, but I need help so get out there."

I quickly finished my oatmeal, grabbed my lunch bag, and started for the door where my mother shoved a bundle of clothing into my arms saying, "Grandpa wants you to take these with you." With both hands full, I rushed out to the barn to helped Grampa finish harnessing Hoss. But first I had to put my spare clothes and lunch on the wagon so they couldn't be forgotten!

After Hoss was harnessed, I was given the task of hooking him to the wagon while Grampa slid the tool box onto the front of the wagon and put the tools for the day and our lunches into it. He put two half-full bags of hay on it, making the seat. I finished hooking up. Grampa checked to see that I had done my job properly. I waved 'bye to Mom. And we were off.

As we plodded along the old roads, sometimes automobiles and occasionally a truck would roar by. It is no distance at all today, going in a car on the same old "back" (now paved) roads we used then. It's about twenty minutes at most. But eight to ten miles behind an old tired horse was a good half day's journey in the old days.

With the old horse's hooves going clipity clop, clipity clop, clipity clop, as even as any metronome, we slowly approached the cider mill. I can still smell the deliciously wonderful aroma of the mill.

The hopper, for grinding the apples (which were first ground to a course pulp before being squeezed in the press), was on the hill close against the back of the mill. We unloaded the apples, bag by bag, at the top of the hill as a man dumped them into the big hopper. The apples were ground in a big machine, fed from the hopper above by gravity.

The ground apples then slid down a chute to the press where the juicy pulp was spread on square forms covered with burlap on the press bed. The top of the press was then brought down on a pile of the forms by a steam ram squeezing the juice out.

The juice from both the grinding mill and the press converged in a tank on the mill's floor, flowing by gravity from the grinder and press into a tank near the loading dock. From there it was piped into the containers down on the loading dock.

After unloading the apples, Grandpa loosened Hoss' harness and hung the nose bag over Hoss' head. We sat on the cool green grass in the shade of a big elm tree having our sandwiches and lemonade. Hoss's lunch was a measure of oats in his nose bag. He ate with relish.

When we finished our lunch, Grampa tightened Hoss' harness and lead him back down the slope around to the front of the mill to the loading dock which was nearly level with the wagon bed. There a man rolled the barrels onto the wagon, and gave each an easy looking flip that stood the barrel on end, and we were ready to go home.

As we plodded along the old roads going home, sometimes automobiles and occasionally a truck, would roar by. One especially noisy truck brought from Grampa, "I 'spose those things will do most of the haulin' from now on. They do go awful fast!"

We got home just before dark. I gave Hoss a drink of water, rubbed him down, and put him in his stall. There, oats, fresh hay and bedding awaited him before we went into the house for our supper.

That was in the late 1920's, probably 1927. I think that was Grampa's last bit of "teaming." It was late summer that I lost my Grampa. Shortly after my fourteenth birthday Grampa and Grama were taking a pleasure ride with their visiting daughter, son-in-law, and granddaughter. The pleasure ride ended suddenly with Grampa having a fatal cerebral hemorrhage.

Everett True grew up on a New England farm where he learned many craft skills. The Agricultural College of Massachusetts taught him to be a florist. The army taught him to keep his head down. After that, to keep his head busy, he took up writing. These vignettes show his grandfather's skill as a teacher in the earlier years.

Fairy Godmother's Night Off

By Mickey Davis

The plan was simple. All I had to do was lose ten pounds and grow three inches by the end of the week.

But I was dismayed when I slipped into my long, slinky black dress on Friday evening. It was still a little snug and even in my highest heels, there was no getting around it — I was still short. The vision in my head of gliding into the Magic Wand Charity Ball, tall and thin, my dress caressing my curves, met harsh reality in the mirror.

"I told you it wouldn't work," my friend and next-door-neighbor Pat said as she combed and sprayed my hair. "You could have eaten all week for what that starving got you."

I sighed, hating to admit she was right. I was going through a serious, early mid-life crisis. This charity ball was my last chance to mix with the beautiful people I had only read about in the newspaper. Never mind that I got the ticket because my boss's wife had to rush home to Detroit to take care of her sick father at the last minute and Mr. Adams had asked — no commanded — that I go in her place.

"These charity affairs are serious business," he had said. "Harlowe Manufacturing needs to be represented and I'm not going by myself. I hate to mingle."

That was an understatement. The office gossip had it that his wife took care of their social obligations. He mostly gritted his teeth, nursed a drink, and put in an appearance.

But here I was, a secretary, invited to socialize with the

rich and famous. I planned to make the most of it. My biological clock was ticking, and even I was asking how come I wasn't married yet. This would be the perfect hunting ground.

"There," said Pat with a final cloud of hair spray. "You look gorgeous."

She turned me to face the mirror, and I had to admit that I did look pretty good. And if I sucked in my stomach, the dress fit perfectly.

"Now, your coach awaits." She bowed low. "Just be sure to be back by midnight, Cinderella — unless, of course, you find something more interesting to do." She gave me a conspiratorial wink.

I thanked her for her help, glad I had a friend like her. Then I climbed into Mabel, my deteriorating carriage, tossing a fast food wrapper onto the floor of the back seat to make room for my evening bag. This Cinderella had to drive herself to the ball.

I could see the lights of the mansion on the hill long before I drove through the big gates and past the gatehouse. As the valet took my keys, the muted sounds of a waltz and the murmur of voices drifted through the open windows. Curtains were pulled back and I could see men in their tuxedos and women in their understated dresses sparkle as they moved.

I handed my invitation to the man at the door (could he really be a butler?), tried not to ogle the immense crystal chandelier that hung in the foyer, and eased my way past the ballroom into a softly lit area humming with genteel conversation. I searched for my boss, Mr. Adams, and found him standing awkwardly near a window, looking as if he would disappear with a frown behind the curtain if anyone spoke to him.

"I see you're finally here," he said, implying that he had been there a while. He looked me up and down, gave a slight grunt, and surveyed the room.

"You should talk to Mrs. Winthrop over there, the one in the brown dress. And Mrs. Graham - I'd like her to know more about the company. She could be useful some day. And don't forget Charles Davenport," he said, nodding in the direction of a group of men. "It's important you talk to him. He is in charge of purchasing for the college."

I was half-tempted to say, "Why don't you do it yourself?"

Instead I asked, "Which one is he?"

"The one with the moustache and the drink in his hand."

I nodded, but wasn't about to join a circle of laughing men.

"Here are some of my business cards. I've got to leave." He backed up slightly as he spoke. "I'm counting on you to do a good job. See you at the office Monday. By the way, nice outfit." With a nod, he was gone.

I watched him flee, thoroughly annoyed. This wasn't the office. I didn't have to do what he said. But then I realized that the only way I had gotten into this mansion to meet people I would never encounter in real life was through the company. I certainly couldn't afford the $250 ticket myself.

I picked up a glass of champagne from a tray carried by a solemn waiter in formal black and white. The candles in the room fluttered as a balmy breeze came through the terrace doors. I looked longingly toward the ballroom, then sighed. Cinderella could go to the ball, but not until she got her chores done. I put the business cards within easy reach in my evening bag, took a deep breath, sucked in my stomach, and eased across the floor as Mrs. Winthrop looked my way.

An hour later, Cinderella was hot and exhausted. I was tired of making small talk, couldn't drink another drop of champagne if I was going to drive home, and my feet in the glass slippers felt like they were on fire. There was more to being a beautiful person than I thought. And I still needed to talk to the elusive Mr. Davenport. I considered skipping it but I knew Mr. Adams would ask me about it on Monday.

Charles Davenport was deep in conversation with a much taller, distinguished-looking man. I hesitated when I heard them discussing electro-something and micro-something else, but really wanted to get the job over with. I joined them, exchanging a few polite words before discussing college purchasing and Harlowe Manufacturing. Finally, Charles Davenport asked me for Mr. Adams' business card and excused himself.

I thought his younger conversation companion was going to leave too, but he turned to me instead.

"Are you as warm as I am?" he asked, unbuttoning his jacket. "I need some air." He motioned for me to join him on the terrace.

I've fulfilled my obligation, I thought as I followed him mechanically through the open doors. I had spoke to everyone I was supposed to and smiled until my cheeks hurt. Finally it was time for me to dance the night away in the ballroom. The only trouble was, all I really wanted to do was go home - to be home, actually, in a hot bath. I considered leaving, but even the thought of walking all the way to the front door and Mabel the Car, and then driving back to my house made my head ache. Five more minutes, I decided, and then I'll go. So much for my happy hunting expedition. I hadn't found Prince Charming; all I had discovered were a lot of boring frogs that I had nothing in common with.

"Doesn't that night air feel great?" said the man next to me as we walked across the stone terrace to the railing. "Mark Miller," he said holding out his hand.

"Abigail Jefferson," I answered, shaking it formally. I was on automatic pilot, about to mention Harlowe Manufacturing and Mr. Adams, as I had so many times this evening, when I decided, the heck with it. I was on my own time and I didn't have to represent anyone. I was just Abby Jefferson, I was tired and I didn't care.

I eased out of my shoes.

"Feet hurt?" he asked.

I nodded, relishing the feel of my stockings on the cool stone.

"Mine too. I'm a tennis shoe man, myself."

I studied him. He must mean tennis shoes like on the tennis court at his country club. He had a nice face, though, white teeth and a mouth that lifted charmingly a little more on one side when he spoke.

I smiled politely. The fresh air was reviving me.

"Do you come to many of these?" I asked, gesturing to include the mansion, the glitter, and the elite.

"Only here," he said with a laugh. "I live in the gatehouse. I'm a teacher," he explained. "High school science." His eyes crinkled nicely at the corners.

"My dad and Old Man Fitzroy were army buddies. He was kind of like an uncle to me when I was growing up."

His strong hand rested casually on the railing. The nails were neatly clipped, but they had traces of grease under them.

He followed my glance and flexed his hand.

"Old Man Fitzroy lets me stay in the gatehouse and I help him out with minor repairs as needed. Tonight the ice machine went on the blink as soon as the first guests arrived." He shrugged. "I'm good at fixing things."

"But I thought you were a guest," I said, eyeing his neatly fitted tux and crisp white shirt.

"Sorry," he shook his head. "I just dressed up to slip in and out, maybe grab a glass of wine and fantasize a little. I was waylaid. I know a few of the people here tonight and

Charles Davenport is especially persistent. He thinks he has a great scientific mind and always wants to "talk shop." Actually you rescued me from him — I was ready to make a break for it."

He gave me a very sexy wink. "Thank you for a most pleasant interruption."

"You're welcome," I said, feeling a little flustered.

We stood in silence, gazing out over the moonlit lawn below. The early summer air softly changed direction and was filled with the fragrance of a million blooming flowers. I took a deep breath and closed my eyes as I enjoyed the perfume.

"Smells good, doesn't it?"

"Incredible," I said, "but where is it coming from?" I looked around the grounds. "I don't see any flowers except the ones inside, and they couldn't possibly smell like this."

Mark Miller gave me an approving smile. "You noticed! Gardening is my hobby and you are smelling my Night-Blooming Cereus. I've been keeping an eye on it and was sure it was going to bloom tonight! In fact, I'm planning to check on it on my way back."

He stepped off the terrace onto the grass and bent down, reaching behind a potted bush. When he straightened, he had a large flashlight in his hand.

"Would you like to see it?" he asked. "It's just on the other side of the hedge. Old Man Fitzroy lets me have a garden to experiment in and this year I've planted a night garden."

I looked back at the lights and the low music, and decided it would be safe to follow him. Other people were milling on the terrace, and a good scream would bring them running. Besides, this Mark Miller seemed like a pretty nice guy.

We slipped through an opening in the hedge and were suddenly in a wonderland. "Do you mind if I turn off the flashlight?" he asked. "It's much prettier in the moonlight."

When the flashlight went out, the garden lit up with a soft glow all its own. I could hear water trickling to one side. The moon was reflected in a small, shimmering pond. "You can see it better from here," he said as he gently took my elbow and steered me to a white cement bench.

I was astonished at what was around me. The garden had a dream-like quality. Dark shadows were everywhere, of course, but white flowers lined the brick path. Patches of white lit up the corners, and assorted, light-colored shapes fluttered as small puffs of wind tickled them.

"It's wonderful!" I whispered.

Mark was delighted at my reaction. "It's the first time I've tried a night garden and you're the first person to see it." I watched him gaze around the enclosed area. "All of the flowers are white and most of them are night-bloomers."

I could feel the tension in my shoulders and back dissolve. I breathed deeply as the breeze ruffled my bangs and the extraordinary perfume again enfolded me.

"That's my Cereus, the Queen of the Night," he said. "Come on. It's over to the side here."

I followed his shadowy shape to a vine climbing near a wall. Even in the moonlight I could see that it held the biggest white flowers I had ever encountered. They were the size of dinner plates and they climbed in a tangle to the top of the wall. In the darkness they looked like Fourth of July fireworks, spectacular in their intricacy. And the smell! It so filled the corner where we stood that I felt dizzy.

"Beautiful, isn't it?" he whispered as we gazed at them together. "But the sad thing is that they bloom for just a single night. By the time the sun comes up tomorrow, all of the blossoms you see here will be dead."

"All of them?"

He nodded. “Too bad, isn’t it. They open around dusk, filling the air with their perfume, only to be gone in the morning. Most people never see them.”

I was enchanted with this hidden garden and the poetic man who had created it. We strolled back to the bench and began to talk. I was comfortable for the first time that evening. The music faded and the voices from the terrace quieted. The lights in the house dimmed and the moon slowly made its was across the sky. Still we talked. Mark and I were old friends getting reacquainted, not strangers making the first awkward attempts at conversation.

As the night chill took over and the moon set, we walked hand in hand to his gatehouse for coffee. Before we knew it, the sky was lightening and there was still more to say. We promised to meet in the evening for dinner.

Dawn peeked through the trees as I walked back past the mystical garden, but I didn’t look at it. The ball was over and the blossoms were gone, but the striking of the midnight chimes or the first rays of the morning sun could not destroy the magic of the night before. Cinderella had found her Prince Charming in the form of a high school science teacher, and even though I had to drive myself home in a sputtering, smoke-belching pumpkin, I knew that the rich and famous had nothing on me. Theirs was a make-believe world. My new one was real.

Jimmy's

by Mickey Davis

Several years ago, if you were to take the road that veered to the right diagonally from Rt. 355, you would have found yourself in the older section of my home town. You would have bumped over the level crossing next to the two-room train station, gone past the old drug store that still had a soda fountain and served pot roast and meat loaf all day, and, if you weren't careful, be out the other side of town before you knew it, missing Jimmy's restaurant altogether.

"Jimmy's" was all it said above the door. The paint was

peeling around the front window that held several hand-lettered signs. The most weather-worn and faded was the one proclaiming, "Today's Special — Turkey." Jimmy loved turkey; he also loved to cook it. So every day his little restaurant was filled with the aroma of roasting turkey.

The place was almost empty the morning I went there on an errand. Of course it was too early for lunch, but the room smelled delicious. Jimmy greeted me with a yell from the back, setting an enormous browned bird on the counter in the kitchen doorway before he came out. He was probably in his seventies or eighties.

"What can I do for ya?" he asked.

"John, over in the coin shop, said he was leaving some papers with you," I answered. "I came to pick them up."

"Got 'em in the office. Be right back." He wiped his hands on his apron and disappeared back into the kitchen.

I looked around. I had heard about Jimmy's. The old timers would come for lunch from the barber shop across the street — the one that still had the red, white, and blue barber pole twirling lazily next to the door. The town police would walk over from the police station for a cup of coffee and a turkey sandwich when they could. Almost everyone who was a native knew about Jimmy's and his good, homemade food.

The dining area wasn't much to look at. The linoleum floor was worn, the walls a nondescript color. A red Formica counter ran down most of one side. Chrome stools with red oilcloth seats popped from the floor in front of it like a row of planted mushrooms, but where a clear plastic box holding donuts and cakes filled the counter top, only the mushroom stems remained — the seats had been removed so no one would sit there.

There were some old chrome and Formica tables here and there in the room. Few of the chairs matched. One table sat in front of the window, but was hidden from the outside by Jimmy's many signs.

High on the wall near the back was a window air conditioner, it's foam-sheet filter tied around the front of it with a piece of string. I wondered how often the health department visited Jimmy's.

Jimmy handed me the envelope and smiled.

"Today's special is turkey!" he said adjusting his suspenders. "Come on back for lunch and give it a try. Made it fresh this morning. Best thing there is."

You won't find Jimmy's down by the train station any more. Maybe he finally retired, or maybe he died — I never heard. For a while the restaurant stood empty, the paper signs continuing to fade and wrinkle in the afternoon sun. I think the ballroom dance studio next door finally took over the space.

They built a big mall a couple of miles north on Rt. 355 — hundreds of stores, eight theaters, probably fifteen chain restaurants. Lots of places to eat, things to do. It's where the action is now.

Most cars head for the mall, bypassing the old town area. The barber shop is still there, although I rarely see anyone in it. The drug store is still there, too, struggling to survive. But if you want some fresh turkey and gravy with homemade mashed potatoes, don't even think about going to the mall. They cut theirs from a turkey loaf, and their mashed potatoes are instant. Jimmy would have shaken his head sadly at that.

So, instead, I like to think of him as cooking up a storm wherever he is.

"What'll it be?" he'll turn to ask with a smile. "The Special today is turkey."

Mickey (Michele) Davis had short stories, poetry and

essays published in Home Life, Mother's Manual, Baby Talk, and other magazines when her children were young. After taking time out to own and manage a restaurant with her husband, begin a computer advertising newsletter, and run her own desktop publishing and mailing services business, she returned to writing. Recently her work and photographs appeared in Mature Living, and her "Life in These United States" entry was published in Reader's Digest.

Doing Your Bit

by Barbara Schrefer

Everyone wondered why she'd married him, but nobody said anything. It wasn't done to discuss things like that. Seemed rude. But she was lovely, my Aunt Florrie, with red gold curls and white skin, and just a few freckles on her nose. She was the star of the show, the spoiled only child, the magnet. In front of her I always stumbled and gawked, twelve years old, terrified of speaking. "And what have you been doing with yourself, Barbara?" she would ask, and I wouldn't be able to think of anything to say, in the end turn away in confusion. What had I been doing with myself? Nothing really, except going to school. What did they expect me to say? I'd chew the end of my plait, turn to my father for help, but he'd just shake his head.

Now, my Uncle Bob was a go-getter, a thin wiry man a head smaller than Florrie. He was no oil painting. My father said he looked like a skinned rabbit, said he could hold him out 'til he frigged to death, and he didn't know why Florrie married him. You see, my father didn't like Uncle Bob, but perhaps that was because Bob was a Catholic, a wicked, sinful, idolatrous papist — I didn't know. It was confusing, the grown-up world.

What I did know was that Bob loved Florrie. He adored, idolized, and treasured her. My mother told me he prayed every night he wouldn't get called up, and paid for masses to be said to get out of being in the army, because he couldn't have borne it if he'd had to leave her. Actually, it was flat feet that did it for him in the end, that and being so small. So he worked himself to death instead selling red petrol, and had some great fiddle with the coupons, my dad said, and made a packet of money on the black market.

After a few months he bought a lovely house for Florrie, overlooking the sea. Florrie didn't have to lift her little finger, and had a woman in to "do" for her. Bob did all the shopping and cooking, even after a hard day's work, and she always said to everyone, "He's the best little husband anyone could have." The only problem for Uncle Bob, so my mother said, was that he was in torment every day because he was jealous of Florrie, jealous of any man looking at her, jealous of the postman, the milkman, the dustbin man, the bus conductor, and the priest who heard her confession. When she went to church, Bob would be outside the confessional straining his ears to find out what she was saying, darting back to his pew when she came out.

Florrie's main love was the piano and she was in the Palm Court Orchestra at the Winter Gardens. Bob couldn't get her to give it up and would stand by her grand piano, part of an adoring group of men, much smaller than the rest of them, looking silly, white-faced with exhaustion after his day's work.

The war dragged on and we all had to do our bit like they said on the wireless. My dad was called up and my mother went into a factory and riveted airplanes, making sure she did a good job so those lovely young men wouldn't come crashing down and lose their lives. I had to carry a gas mask all the time in a brown cardboard case that got soggy when it rained. We spent some nights in the Anderson shelter, but it didn't bother me much because my mum was there and so everything was all right.

We wondered, sometimes, what was going on at Uncle Bob's. Had he managed to pull strings and get Florrie out of doing her bit? We didn't have a car or telephone, and the trains were taken up by soldiers, so the only way you could find out anything was by letter, and you couldn't write down something like that, couldn't say, "How are you, Florrie, have you been doing your bit, or has Bob got you out of it?"

Quite a long time went by and then, one day, when I got home from school, who should I see in the front parlor, talking to my mother, but Uncle Bob. I'd caught sight of him through the window and gone running up to wave at him, but when I saw that he was crying and his big nose was bright red, and his face all screwed up I drew back. After that I took a peep and saw that his shoulders were shaking, his hands twisting his big white hanky into a rope. My mother caught my eye and made a big shooing motion with her arms, like I was a goose, and I slunk round the back and into the kitchen.

They seemed to be in there for hours. I was starving hungry but daren't get anything to eat — my mother had our rations worked out down to the last crumb and I would have caught it good and proper if I'd taken anything.

Finally I heard some shuffling and more sobbing, and my mother's voice syrupy and comforting, "There, there, Bob, don't take on so, it'll all blow over, it's the war, you know," and then the front door shutting quietly.

"Oh, what a to-do this is," she said coming into the kitchen, wringing her hands on her apron. "That poor fellow's just about off his head."

"What's up, Mum?" I asked.

"None of your business," she said. "You're too young to understand this lot, but I'll tell you something, that Florrie never was any good for him, she thinks because she plays the piano she's better than the rest of us. She doesn't even put up her raspberries and he's grown 'em for her special and all." She glared at me as though it was my fault, then cut me a piece of bread, spread it with margarine, thought for a moment, scraped off half the margarine, and smeared it on another piece.

Shortly after that we got a card in the post. It said a son had been born to Florrie and Robert, 8 lbs 10 ozs.. My mother didn't look very pleased though, or knit anything and send it, and I thought it a bit queer, but daren't say anything.

When my dad came home on leave, I knew the story would come out. I knew my mother would tell him what had gone on after I had gone to bed, so I wrapped myself in a blanket, crept halfway down the stairs to the exact spot where I knew I could hear but not be seen, if the door opened, and waited.

After a while, my father said, "What's going on with your Robert, then? How did he manage to get a bun in Florrie's oven? He must have had the Archangel Gabriel come down and give him a lift. I didn't think he had it in him, to tell you the truth."

Don't be like that, George," said my mother. "That poor fellow has been through the torments of hell itself. It's his own fault for marrying someone with red hair, though. I knew no good would come of it."

"What I don't understand," said my father, "is what he sold that lovely big house for, I mean having a baby and all you'd think they'd be needing more room, not less. I can't believe it's because they're short of money. He'll always have a bob or two, that one, and there's nothing gone wrong with the black market as far as I can see."

"Oh, I have a proper tale to tell you, George. There's a lot you don't know. Poke the fire and I'll make a cup of tea, then I'll get going with the story."

I had to sit, then, on the freezing stairs, listening to the settling coals, the rattling cups and saucers and the hissing of boiling water being poured into the tea pot.

"Well, this is what happened," said my mother, finally. "About six months ago I'd just got back from the shops when I saw Robert getting off the bus at the corner. Seven hours it'd taken him to get here from Morecambe, you know what busses are like, these days."

"Get on with it," said my dad.

"Well, it turns out that the War Office sent them a letter saying that Florrie had to do something — something apart from playing the piano and looking like Rita Hayworth after she'd had her hair done, that is. Seems Florrie had a choice. She could work in the factory like me — can you imagine it, Miss High and Mighty getting them long red nails round a riveting gun — or she could take in evacuees, or they could have a soldier billeted on them. They thought about the evacuees, but you never know what you're getting, you know. Some of them children have nits in their hair, and sore ears, and Mrs. Dryden got two who'd never used a knife and fork before, at least that's what she said, and she couldn't get them clean — they had tides round their necks you couldn't scrub off — and they had infections, too."

"What's this got to do with Florrie?"

"I'm telling you. What they finally decided was to have a soldier; he would be out most of the time and he could have his own room and keep to himself."

"Oh aye, so what went wrong?"

"What went wrong? I'll tell you what went wrong. First off, he looked like Tyrone Power, that's what went wrong. On top of that, he's an officer with a posh voice like he went to public school, with lovely manners and our Robert only came up to his chest, and this officer — Brian something his name was — took one look at Florrie and they clicked. He didn't seem to go out at all, even spent his leave at Robert's house. That's when our Robert really twigged something was going on.

"He was always the jealous kind, your Robert. What did he do about it?"

"What could he do? He suffered torments, that's what he did. This fellow Brian started cooking for her and bringing wine home, and you know Bob can't drink that fancy foreign stuff, it upsets his stomach something terrible. And this Brian and Florrie always had their heads together, laughing, and she starts wearing some French-sounding scent, and painting her toe nails red, and I don't know what else. Our Bob used to come running home at all times, moidered to death about what was going on, and frightened to death of finding out. Anyhow, you know what happened next, don't you?"

"No, what did happen?"

"You great lummox, what do you think? She tells Bob she's expecting, that's what. And he turns into a madman, throwing pots around, and pans and even some of his Crown

Derby china — and you know how much that costs, not that you can get it anymore with the war and all."

"He threw his Crown Derby around?

"Yes, that's how upset he was, and she's crying, and he's crying, and the soldier, what does he do, he asks to be billeted somewhere else — unfavorable conditions — that's what he said. Anyway, after a lot of hargy bargy, Bob said he'd forgive her and bring up the child."

"How did he know it wasn't his?

"How do you think he knew it wasn't his, you stupid buggar."

"Oh aye, I see what you mean," said my dad, after a minute.

"Well, the next news is the War Office said they had to take in another soldier because they had all that room. But Bob said he wasn't having any — you know how wily he can be — so he sold that lovely house and now they are living in a row house in a back street with an outside lavatory and two miserable little bedrooms, not even a bathroom. No room for any soldiers in there. Those houses should have been condemned, that's what I say.

"But do you know what I think, George," she continued, "I think that's how Bob's punishing her. I don't think they'll ever leave that back street, not ever, she'll be living there 'til she dies, and Robert doesn't care — he'll keep her a prisoner in that little house forever and a day."

"I reckon you're right, Alice," my father said with a sigh.

I carefully, on hands and knees, got to the top of the stairs, then pulled my frozen body into bed, lying shivering under the sheets, thinking about Auntie Florrie. It reminded me of a story I'd heard once, about a man walling up his wife in a castle while she was alive because she'd been unfaithful to him, and leaving her there to die .

My mother was right, they never did leave the little house. Many of the surrounding back streets were torn down for slum clearance, but for some reason that street remained standing.

The boy grew into a big, tall, excessively handsome young man who looked remarkably like Tyrone Power. It's funny, isn't it, people whispered, that a little runty fellow like Bob has such a big, fine lad for a son.

As her child grew, Florrie seemed to shrink. The red hair faded, the piano was sold. I once heard her say, in a sad moment, "It was the war, you know, the terrible war. That was the cause of it all. It wouldn't have happened if I hadn't had to do my bit."

Barbara Schrefer was born in Lancashire, England in the 1930's. She has memories of a World War 11 childhood. In her twenties she lived in London and Paris. In the early '60's she came to America, and has lived in New York, San Francisco and Washington D.C.

In 1990 she received the Maryland State Arts Council Individual Artist Award in Fiction; and in 1991 won first place in the Florida State Writing Competition - novel category - sponsored by the Florida Freelance Writers Association. She recently won second place for Fiction - Literary Short Story in the Florida Freelance Writers Association Competition. She is now completing her third novel.

At the present time she lives in Clearwater, Florida.

Breath Sounds

by L. Shaw Blimes

The old woman lay in bed and listened to the raspy, rhythmical sound of the old man's breathing. What will it be like, she wondered when I listen and hear only silence? What will I do? How will I feel? Will it be worse, or will it be better? At least it will be different, and maybe just being different will make it better. For fifty years now she had been waking up to the sound of his breath. Fifty years was a very long time.

The sun peered around the edges of the window shade. She rose quietly from beneath the comforter careful not to waken him, and pushed her bare toes into the slippers that waited under the bed. Her feet made a soft, padding sound as she walked down the hallway to the bathroom door.

She washed her wrinkled face and ran a comb through her thin gray hair, remembering how it used to shine in the sun when she was young and it was thick and dark. She hurried into the kitchen to start the coffee. If she was lucky, she would be able to get a piece of toast eaten before he called to her.

No toast today. Not right now, anyway. From the bedroom came the quiet thud of his heavy cane hitting the floor. It was his way of summoning her when he couldn't make her hear his withering voice.

She stopped before entering the room, taking a moment to make herself smile. She wanted to smile because she remembered what it was like to love him. But that memory had gotten tangled in the very back of her mind and she couldn't seem to find the key that would bring it forward. It was trapped there somewhere, wedged between the images of love songs, long walks and shared laughter. All that was so long ago. She smiled because this was her life now, and she had to.

"Good morning, Thomas" she said, entering the room. She leaned across the bed greeting him with a kiss. But there was no remembered passion, there wasn't even sweetness. There was just the habit of the morning kiss. It doesn't matter she thought, he doesn't know the difference anyway. She opened the window shade, helped him to sit up and struggled to get him onto his feet. She guided him to the chair in the living room, turned on the TV and gave him the remote then returned to the bedroom to smooth the comforter and empty the plastic urinal that sat on the night stand.

This morning, like every morning, breakfast was coffee, eggs, toast and the required medications. She knew how to place everything on the tray so it would balance just right as she brought it to where he sat with the remote still in his hand. There was no thank you. His eyes remained on the dancing colors of the television screen.

"Don't forget to wipe your mouth," she told him, taking the remote. She placed the paper napkin in his hand and squeezed until his unwilling fingers gave way and held it on their own. Life is so unkind, she thought. He turned from the TV and smiled at her, but his brown eyes showed no hint of recognition and watching him she could find no hidden trace of the young man she once loved so dearly. She longed to see him, even if just for a second. But he was gone. Dead and buried in a shallow grave covered with the dirt of stroke and illness.

At 10 a.m. he dozed in the chair. Once again, the sucking, whispering voice of his breath sounds filled the room. She escaped on tiptoe out into the sun to visit the mailbox and see what junk-mail treasures waited there. A large, white envelope was carefully wedged in the box. It was addressed "To: Mom and Dad" in the handwriting of her daughter.

She remembered the day, five years ago when her daughter had loaded the boys into the car, kissed her good-bye and moved to the West Coast. Except for the image of the tearful farewell, which was burned into her memory, and a few wedding pictures when her older grandson married, she hadn't seen them since. Occasionally, late at night, she would imagine what it would be like to board a plane and fly off for a visit. But Thomas could not make the trip, and she could not spread her wings as long as Thomas was grounded. Even the younger boy must be strong and tall by now. He would be graduating from high school soon. Maybe this year, maybe next, she couldn't remember exactly when.

The words "Photos - Do Not Bend" were scribbled in bright red letters across the front of the envelope. Pictures she thought, her mood brightening, probably of the great-grandbaby. She crept back into the house and sat down at the kitchen table. From the other room came a sound of gurgling, and she paused, listening; hoping she would not have to get up and shake the old man. She recalled the way she shook her children when they were sleeping infants and she was afraid for them. A gentle, loving shake that said, "Don't go. I need you. You've just gotten here and life holds magic moment's for us to share."

The breathing became regular again. She slid her knotted finger under the sealed flap of the envelope and pulled upward, tearing the paper. She drew the picture from its hiding place and her eyes fell across the glossy surface.

"Thomas!" His name buzzed through her lips, pushed out by surprise and pleasure. The image that smiled up at her was the old man, now young again; Thomas at eighteen when they first met. That was his face, handsome and strong. The tangle of memories in her mind suddenly broke, and in that moment she inhaled the spicy fragrance of his aftershave, felt his hand firm around her waist as they danced on their wedding night and knew once more the softness of his lips gently touching her own. "Thomas," she caressed the captured likeness, rubbing it against her cheek, then holding it down again to run her fingers along the photo trying to absorb every youthful feature: the high forehead, the Roman nose, the blue eyes...

From the recliner in the living room came the bubbling sounds of moist breathing. Then silence. She dropped the picture of her grandson on the table, and hurried to Thomas to give him a little shake. The kind she used to give her children when they were infants, and she was afraid for them. A gentle, loving shake that said, "Don't go. I need you. You've just gotten here and life still has magic moments for us to share."

Here Comes the Bride

by L. Shaw Blimes

"You want what?" I asked trying to make my voice sound more like a purr than a growl.

"Mom, hang on. I have a call on the other line. I'll be right back ." Click, silence. White lace, satin and sequins; that was what I pictured when Valarie announced she and Jason were planning to be married. White lace, satin and sequins was what every mother of the bride envisioned and every father of the bride willingly opened the check book to provide.

I remembered when she first called to say he had proposed. "Mom," she breathed into the phone. "Jason asked me to marry him. He took me to the Kahiki and right there in front of everyone in the restaurant, he got down on one knee and asked me to be his wife. He cried, I cried and a cute gray-haired couple at the table next to us kept giving him a thumbs up." It seemed a romantic beginning to a wedding celebration. Just what I expected.

The date was set for October. Six months was a comfortable length of time to plan the wedding I had dreamed of since the day she was born. We would spend time pouring over books of beautifully engraved invitations, stopping for a late lunch before running to the florist. She with eyes bright and sparkling, me with the quiet smile of a proud and benevolent matriarch.

There would be many visits to bridal boutiques. This gown, layered with Chantilly lace might seem just perfect until she tried the next one. In it, she would look like a princess. Even Cinderella would be jealous. In my musings, I could almost hear the rustle of satin and netting as she pulled each dress over her head, trying not to let it drag across a fitting room floor specked with lint and sprinkled with straight pins.

My veil! The picture came of rice thrown toward my veil with her face beneath it. If she chose the right dress, I could suggest she use it.

Only a few days after setting the October date she had called again, to make a second announcement. "We've decided on a small ceremony. Since Jason graduates in May, we thought it would be more logical to be married by then. That way he's not limited to considering jobs only in this area. We've moved the date up. We're getting married on April 27th !" Crash! Boom! Shattered were all my thoughts of gowns and florists and leisurely luncheons.

"April 27th," I repeated the date, giving my mind time to clear the debris of my vanished dream and do the mathematical calculations. "That's only three weeks from now!" My heart knew the truth. Weddings were supposed to be based on fairy tale and fantasy, not logic.

"I know," she sang happily into the phone. "That's why we've decided on a small ceremony."

So much for white lace, satin and sequins. They went up in flames quickly once the bride put a match to them! But mothers don't surrender their dreams easily. So the thought returned to me, if she chooses a pretty white lace dress, my veil might still work.

Click. She was back on the line. "Mom, are you here? Now, where were we?" Her voice was filled with excitement and I knew she was smiling. Caught up in her happiness, I instinctively returned that smile, although only to the unseeing face of the telephone receiver. "Darn, there's the other line again. Sorry..."

The phone-line silence pushed my mind back to the settling smoke of satin, sequins and lace. Eventually, the veil, too, was replaced when she found a perfect little pale yellow dress with tiny periwinkle-colored flowers that matched the blue in her eyes. She loved it, and because she loved it I had known instantly that I would love it, too. But it just didn't go with a veil. A flower for her hair. That would be much more "Valarie" than my veil.

She hadn't chosen white lace, she hadn't chosen satin and she hadn't chosen sequins.

She hadn't dreamed my dream at all. She had her own. But still, I could see that in her dream there was a special place for a proud and benevolent matriarch. One who would watch, with a quiet smile as her child became both a wife and a woman.

Click. "Mom?"

"I'm here for you Sweetie, like I always have been and I always will be. Now, what great idea did you want to talk to me about?"

L. Shaw Blimes was born and raised in the central Ohio area. She attended both Ohio State University (Columbus, Ohio) and Brigham Young University (Provo, Utah) studying elementary education and dabbling in creative writing. After raising a family of five children, she and her husband, David, moved to Tarpon Springs, Florida, where Ms. Blimes settled in and began to follow her life's dream of writing stories on themes of special interest to women.

Sacrifice on Manitoualin

by Mary T. Dresser

Alex Grant, a Scots-African spy in the American Revolution, has been sent by George Washington to explore the Northwest Territory acquired in the peace with Britain. Washington wants to keep slavery from the new lands. Alex, whom the Indians call "Many Wounds," is saved from death by the medicine woman, Kwana. She believes the spirit Nanabozho requires a warrior sacrifice.

Chapter Ten of the novel FREEDOM'S COST.

The canoes entered a bay off Lake Huron on the southwest side of Manitoualin Island and sped toward the yellow beaches. Pines were green on the bluff and the sun sparkled on the clear water. No people were visible.

The bottom of the bay was transparent beneath their paddles as they glided in. Alex watched the sleek muscles in Stephen's back stretch long and the paddle dip eagerly as they shot across the surf.

"What do you seek on Manitoualin, Stephen?" he asked as the canoe crunched into the sand. He was irritated at himself for not asking sooner.

"I have a wife and two children here," Stephen answered, eagerness in his voice.

So Mary Brant had sent Stephen home to Manitoualin because she didn't want a man in her bed who was longing for his wife. Wise woman. Alex ignored the apprehension that was tugging at his consciousness like an importunate child. Something dangerous awaited him. The thought of wife and home and family seemed to wander aimlessly in his mind without finding a refuge. Perhaps it was the residual effect of the medicine potions he had been given. Kwana was next to him, dragging the paddle, her bronze skin and all her naked flesh gleaming in the sunshine.

From the thick wooded forest they could hear the furtive movement of animals. The island was silent except for the raucous calls of crows and ravens circling in the sky. The black eaters of the dead seemed in no hurry. They were waiting for their opportunity and the flesh crawled on his arms.

When they leapt from the boats, Kwana called the warriors to stand before her and Alex could see she was anxious. She begged for blessing from the spirit Nanabozho who had created Michillimakinac and Manitoualin. She swept her arms open to the sky and arched her back until her black hair dragged in the sand. None could understand the words she was saying. Finally she straightened and faced her people.

"This is the man of my medicine dream," she said to them as they muttered softly. "I was told in the dream that he is the one sent to satisfy the evil on Manitoualin, since none of our people will please Nanabozho. It is why I saved this American from the knife. This man—a warrior— must go forth for us all. He is our gift to the spirit, Nanabozho, who made the island. Nanabozho will take our offering."

She stepped forward, took the knife of manhood from his waist and untied his loincloth. Then she removed the vest, displaying his old scars and the new ones she had inflicted. She took paint from her medicine bag and smeared the crimson and ocher grease over his chest and painted black across his face. It was the Indian mark of death. From her pack she took the Purple Heart he had thought lost and hung it around his neck.

"This is the medicine of your people," she said and he saw that her eyes were swimming with tears. "For the people of the tribes, I have painted your tattoos. The Spirit gives you the honor of scars, Many Wounds. We are giving Nanabozho a brave warrior."

The last months with the tribesmen had separated him from the world of history and poetry and art—almost like a flaying—and nothing remained but the beating of his heart and the memory of those he loved. And, perhaps, loyalty to his clan.

"I will go but send my people home," he told her and she nodded solemnly. He knew that, to her, it was his last request because she did not expect him to return.

Stephen stood beside him and said he was an Oneida warrior and demanded the right to keep the American captain company. Kwana refused, shaking her head fiercely and biting her lips. Stephen was gripped solidly by several braves. Then Dan and Noey moved forward and Alex put up his hand to halt them. He walked away from Kwana and stood alone, feeling bereft of all human love.

"I am not tied like an animal," he said to the Indians. "Your sacrifice is only worthy if I walk across the beach by myself. Take your hands from my friends. They are to be respected."

The warriors moved back from Stephen who stood tall before them, his arms crossed, his eyes pleading. Alex shook his head in denial.

"You can't go, Stephen," he said. "Thank you but stay here and help my friends get back to Philadelphia."

"Captain Grant," Dan said in English. "Don't go up there. We can fight. We've got our muskets."

"Against fifty?" he asked. "If I don't return who knows what will happen? There are probably warriors up there among the trees. You may have to fight hundreds here on the beach. You'll need these Ottawa warriors on your side. Start loading the muskets now. Live to get back to the General."

She had taken his moccasins and the sand was burning his bare feet as he turned and walked toward the silent bluff. He could feel the warriors watching him stoically as he started up the incline. Kwana in her golden skin glory stood before them, holding his breech cloth in her hands. He was naked and free. He was purged of all but his own fire of life.

Primitive, he thought. The Knight goes into battle, while the demure and pure maiden waits. Such a maiden. Damn it. He was an educated man, a teacher, a linguist, a sly and careful spy. A married man with a child. They were treating him as if he were Theseus being sacrificed to the Minotaur. These Indians were as uncivilized as the early Greeks. There is nothing up here in the shadows under the trees but a tribe of savages, intent on taking my scalp. At least it should be quick—no slow torture or flaying.

"Though I walk through the valley of the shadow of death,
I will fear no evil,
Because Thy rod and Thy staff they comfort me."

He repeated the words over and over. The twenty-third psalm seemed a place of rescue, far from the madness of a savage world that had swallowed him.

His heels crunched in the last of the sand and now he was into the pine grove and pine needles spiked his feet. The ravens were cawing and wheeling in the sky and the bushes and trees rustled in a faint August breeze.

Accepting fate did not mean surrender. He knew why he was being sent into this unknown terrain, why he had been preserved from a tortured death by Kwana, protected and pampered by her. He was a black man, different from the rest. He had been different in Philadelphia and in Paris. All his life he had been forced to be alone. Even his mother had deserted him. Now, because they believed he did not belong to any tribe, he was the victim selected to die for people he did not know.

They were wrong. He was a Grant. An American. And a man, God damn it. Kwana had taken his small knife. He picked up several rounded stones at his feet. He was not a captive slave. He would fight.

All about him the thick underbrush was stirring and he could hear impatient animals twitching and breathing. A vile smell drifted to him on the sticky air.

"Monstrum horrendum, informe, ingens, cui lumen ademptum," he said, grimly, flaunting his mordent humor in the face of terror. "Virgil, my students," he muttered: *"A monster frightful, shapeless, huge, bereft of sight."*

Now he could see the Amikwa village. There was no palisade, just three longhouses. The place was deserted except for a few raccoons that dashed through the pathways and scurried away when they saw him. Maybe the Amikwa left some weapons behind when they vanished. He hurried toward the first longhouse and then halted in fear, his heart pounding. The deer hide door cover was billowing as if some creature were straining to be out.

He heard himself scream in horror when a red-eyed black dog burst forth, dragging the body of a baby. When he threw a rock at the dog, the animal dropped its dreadful burden and sped into the underbrush, howling. He pitched the rest of the rocks in the dog's direction. The infant's corpse lay at his feet, gray-green and decomposing.

He stepped over the child that lay like a ruined toy at the door of the longhouse and tore back the hide door. The stench of death, pestilence and decay hit him like the devil's burden and made him reel back against the door frame.

The Amikwa longhouse usually held a dozen families. All along the walls, in their allotted spaces, were the bed rolls, pallets, fur blankets, and cradleboards of the tribe, while on these bits of native life lay the putrefying bodies of their owners. Women, children, men—some with clothing torn off in a last agony—lay exposed, faces and bodies ravaged with pustules. Maggots and worms were crawling across faces and into open mouths.

He staggered out the door and retched. Crows were now swooping lower, attempting to fly into the carrion house. There were at least thirty people dead in the one longhouse. All victims of smallpox.

Kwana's dream was right. He was the only one who could go into the evil she saw on Manitoualin Island. Alex had survived smallpox when he was five years old. The disease was particularly virulent among the Indian tribes. Some whites and Negroes seemed to have enough immunity to survive, but the pox was wiping out the Indian race faster than rifles.

He forced himself upright and staggered back toward the longhouse, cursing himself for his weakness. Grabbing a scrap of woven fabric that hung forlornly near the doorway, he covered his mouth and nose and took shallow breaths as he staggered from body to body. All must be dead, he told himself until he reached a pallet half way through the longhouse and a child began to wail. She was about ten years old and covered with pustules, some oozing, some dry. When she yelped like a small animal, he took her in his arms and rushed outside.

He laid her beneath a wide shade tree and went to the water cask beside the door. It was slimed with dead bugs but he scooped deep with the gourd and produced lukewarm life. Holding it to her broken lips, he said, "You can live. I did." The child rolled her eyes and he covered her with leaves and scraps from the hide door cover. He fought off the crows before re-entering the longhouse.

This time, he looked diligently for life in the three houses that made up the village. He found an old woman, an emaciated young warrior and a boy of about four. The brave was hard to drag but the woman and child were easier. He laid them out together beneath the tree, next to the girl.

Squatting beside them, he tried to plan what to do. He knew enough about smallpox from Doctor Franklin and Madam Stewart to realize that these survivors were contagious. Even the clothing a smallpox victim wore could transmit the disease. The dead could kill the living. He hurried back into the longhouse and brought out robes and blankets to cover them. The blankets were contaminated with the plague, but so was he.

The books had told him what had been done in the Old World when the Black Plague struck. They had boarded up the victims in their houses and left them to die. This was a modern time. Martha had said plagues were spread, not by people but by propinquity and filth. The disease had to be excoriated through cleanliness.

He ran to the fire wheel beside the door and began to stir the spark. When it caught he inserted twigs, and fire kindled.

"The beginning and the end," he muttered. "Alpha and Omega."

He shoved a burning brand onto the side of the birch longhouse. It flared and he ran to fire the next corner. Then he set fires in the other two houses. Within moments, the dry longhouses were funeral pyres for people he only knew as a tribe called Amikwa.

The old woman, propped against the roots of a tree, opened her blood-engorged eyes and said, in the Algonquian tongue, "You are making my house dirty."

"I am sorry, Mother," Alex said, his voice erratic. "I will

make good any disturbance I have caused."

"You should," she said. "My son will punish you."

"I will accept his correction," Alex said, and she dropped her face onto her chest and slept.

"Poor bastard died before she could instruct him," he muttered to himself as he staggered down the bluff toward the beach. He was not the sacrifice because the pox would not kill him. The Indians, his men, and Kwana would be the sacrificial victims if he could not teach them.

Kwana was kneeling before the canoes keening a death song while the warriors stood beside her like a Greek chorus. When he emerged from the trees, she opened her arms to him as if she were accepting the arrival of Zeus.

He dodged her and ran into the waters that lapped against the shore. Running deeper and deeper into the bay, he dove into the waves and tried to cleanse himself. He pulled the eel skin from his topknot and let his hair flow free and rubbed the paint from his face and chest.

As he ducked and scrubbed at his body, Kwana came out into the water to stand before him.

"Keep away!" he shouted.

"You live, Many Wounds," she said. "My dream of death was wrong."

He stood up, water flowing from his face.

"You were right about death, Kwana," he said. "Do you see the fire?"

She whirled and gazed in awe at the black cloud that was rolling above the tree line.

"The bodies of the people, the Amikwa, are going in that smoke. They have died of the pox. If you want to save the lives of the people on the beach, you must make the warriors obey me."

She nodded her head as if she were a child agreeing to a discipline.

"First, you must tell them that the pox is so deadly that it will kill them if they touch a victim or the clothing of a victim. That is why I burnt the longhouse. They may build lodges for themselves but each lodge must be for only one person. A longhouse helps spread the disease. They must wash in these waters three times a day. Any contact with people who are dying may kill them."

"Are all the Amikwa dead, Many Wounds?" she asked.

"There are four alive on the bluff. I must bring them down. Have the warriors build a long house for them. Please, make the warriors obey me, Kwana. As a child, I survived the pox. I will try to save them. And you. It is your only chance."

Sunlight bounced off the waters as she bowed to him and turned back toward shore. The ravens were cawing their irritation while they circled above the smoke. As she walked from the water, he thought that the sleek line of her body was as smooth as an otter. He dove down, holding his breath until his chest ached.

Kwana called the warriors together on the beach before he returned. They stood before him as he strapped on his loincloth and climbed onto the side of an overturned canoe. He tried to speak in their language while translating, again, for his own men. Dan, Noah and Stephen were standing close together while Simon MacCauly was alone, fingering his musket and glaring at the group.

"Warriors," Alex said, forcing his voice to reach them. "I have returned from death. The Amikwa have the pox that came into the land with the white men. All the Amikwa were dead in their longhouse accept for four I have saved. Have any of you, here, suffered from the pox?"

There was silence from the throng. Simon MacCauly raised one hand and Alex understood his need for a sandy beard to cover the scars. Stephen raised his hand, hesitantly. He was half-French.

"We must care for the survivors," Alex said. "We must also go to all the other Amikwa settlements on Manitoualin Island and see if any live. Tonight all must sleep alone. Outside. Under the canoes. Under bushes. First, we must make a longhouse for the pox survivors. No one shall go into that longhouse except myself. Tomorrow, I will send Stephen and Simon to look for the people on the rest of the island. Simon and I must go now to bring back the survivors from the village."

The warriors began to debate among themselves as Kwana moved between groups, talking and listening. It occurred to Alex that it had been better when she wore medicine paint. Now she looked too much like a woman. Hands thrust out at her and she moved like quicksilver, dodging between tribal groups.

Simon MacCauly strode up to him and stood with his hands folded across his chest.

"You and I and that one Indian are the only ones who have a chance of living through the summer," he said. "General Washington asked if I were immune before he sent me."

"He understands such things," Alex said. "He suffered the pox when he was young."

"We should leave now," MacCauly said. "Most of them are probably dead and don't know it. I have maps. Let us take a canoe and go while they are still in shock."

"What about Dan and Noey?" Alex asked, leaning back against the canoe and breathing deep.

"We take them before they are infected. They don't deserve to die here."

"These people, the Amikwa, the Ottawa, the Wyandotte, the Oneida. They don't deserve to die either. We must help. Follow me up the hill to bring down the people."

"You are a fool," MacCauly said, and looked upward toward the bluff. "Or maybe you are smart. Bring them down and they can infect the rest. Good—and we will be rid of the whole crowd."

"We must do it," Alex said, "They are alive."

"And what has the big woman offered to give you as a reward, Captain?" MacCauly asked, turning, his eyes narrowed. "I hear squaws like to service buck niggers."

Alex walked away from MacCauly, his hand tight on the hilt of his hunting knife. Several of the men had heard the tone of the insult and some began to walk toward them in barely concealed anticipation of a fight that would permanently still MacCauly's caustic voice. They were smiling eagerly as Alex seriously considered this option. However, he needed MacCauly's help in a formidable job. Lives were at stake and he could not let them pay the cost of his injured self-esteem.

Stephen was coming towards him slowly, shoulders sagging like an old man.

"Did you have a son about four or a daughter about ten, Stephen?" Alex asked. The man shook his head, agony in his eyes. Stephen had lost his entire family and they hadn't known he was coming for them. Alex could not permit him to see what remained of the village.

"The fire is sending their souls to the God in Heaven," Alex said, pointing at the black smoke. "Our priests tell us those we love wait for us there."

"Did your God send the pestilence?" Stephen asked, hoarsely.

"I don't know. But He gave us minds so we can try to fight it. Help with building shelters and saving others. That must be why we are all here. Come, Mr. MacCauly. I hear you are a Christian. Let the pagans see you act on it."

They carried one canoe up the bluff and Alex and MacCauly loaded the pox survivors into it. Then they pushed the canoe down through the soft sand. By the time they reached the beach, the warriors had finished assembling a rough bark lodge. Alex ordered them to move far away and turned to making the four sufferers comfortable. MacCauly did not deign to remove the disgust from his face but he was deft and they managed to clean the people and give them some water before falling exhausted onto the mud floor.

The old woman recovered quickest. In the morning she wakened Alex by standing above his blanket and poking his ribs with her feet. Her deerskin smock was bedraggled, her white hair tangled on her head, and she was picking at the scabs on her face. She was also talking. This, he was to learn, was her constant activity.

She told him her name was Bright Dawn and she was fifty summers old. When he explained that her son was among those who died of the pox she stood silent for some minutes.

"I am sorry, Bright Dawn," Alex said, rising to stand before her. She frowned at him, which was a truly ghastly thing on a face haggard from fever and newly pockmarked. She asked his name and then examined his body, checking under his loincloth, using her fingers to trace the tattoos and turning his hands over several times.

"I have had the pox, so I will not get it again," he reassured her and she nodded. "Neither will you."

"Braid your hair," she said. "And obtain some meal and beef so I can cook. You are thin but strong, so you should live long. You need new moccasins. Do you have a mother?"

"No, Bright Dawn," he said, inching his way toward the lodge entrance.

"Now you have one," she said and patted him firmly on his bare rump.

He washed himself in the lake and tied his hair back with the eel strap while musing about the resiliency of women. After sending MacCauly and Stephen off to find if any life still existed along the coves and small lakes of Manitoualin, he supervised the warriors in building rude bark lodges in the sand or in the shelter of the bluff. Kwana was working beside them, now wearing her paint and a loincloth. She helped them build her a small dome-shaped lodge near the water's edge.

Many of the Ottawa said they wished to sleep under their canoes and he did not object. Long Stroke intended to make a few more trade stops at the islands around Manitoualin, St. Ignace, and the Fort. Then it would be time to turn south. No one wished to stay on the island or be on Lake Huron when September came.

He sent Dan and Noah with Long Stroke and returned to his nursing duties. The four Amikwa were recovering, which was good because, within six days, MacCauly and Stephen arrived with ten more survivors in the canoe.

Stephen and Alex carried the sick into the lodge while MacCauly rushed off to cleanse himself.

When MacCauly rejoined them, Alex told Stephen to wash himself until his skin fell off and ordered MacCauly to assist him with the sick. Bright Dawn was bustling around the lodge and lecturing the newcomers on hygiene and the strength and the powerful genitalia of her new son with the brown skin who had saved them all. It comforted Alex that MacCauly could not understand the Algonquian tongue.

The Amikwa brave died suddenly and they lost a child the first night but a dozen were alive after a week. It took that long before he could finally rest in a shaded spot outside the hospital longhouse and smoke his pipe. He was on a long sail into the unknown and some God or Devil had thrown away the tiller.

No place was solitary on the beach at Manitoualin Island. Kwana stood above him and he looked up. Her body was painted but not her face.

"I am here for you. If you wash and strip off your clothing you will not infect me," she said. "I would come to you and give you pleasure."

"I am married. My wife is named Maureen," he said and she walked away. Her buttocks were smooth, as gracefully rounded as the curve of the headland framing the bay and her legs were long and flowing with energy and taut muscle.

Entranced, he did not immediately see the canoes coming into the bay. They were Ottawa and when he finally rose to meet them he saw Long Stroke and Dan at the prow paddles.

Behind them was a chunky man in buckskins with black curled hair and beard, a wide nose, and dark skin. He was out of the canoe before it reached shore, striding across the beach to embrace Alex enthusiastically.

"Mon cher," the man exclaimed. "You are the black Scotsman sent from General Washington. I am Jean Baptiste Pointe du Sable. Welcome. Be elated. I have had the pox. But many of the British in Fort Mackinac have not. They are dying beautifully."

Mary T. Dresser is the author of two unpublished novels set in the American Revolutionary period, STAND FAST and FREEDOM'S COST. She has also completed four novels about the late Roman Empire in Britain. Trained as a Journalist, she has thirty-five years experience as a writer and editor for newspapers, magazines and television in Chicago, Washington, D.C., and Florida.

Nonfiction

The Great Muscovy Caper

or

A "bird in the hand" is messy, indeed

by Belva Green

My house is on a quiet canal that leads to a small lake. I have a dock, no boat. Around many of our lakes in Florida, Muscovy ducks are nuisance wild ducks. Florida has a sizable population. Usually they are ugly birds in a variety of colors — red heads, green, black and white bodies — raggedy feathers. The two that frequented my area were, I thought, rather attractive. I liked them. To me, they looked cheerful; their eyes seemed to smile.

And when the mother Muscovy appeared proudly trailing seven tiny fluffies, I made sure they had a pan of milk and lots of cracked corn and bread crumbs. She was so appreciative and enthusiastic that I was sorry to notice that apparently one of the lake's alligators had devoured two of the ducklings.

The five survivors grew fast. Finally, I stopped feeding them because they got to be a nuisance. They became a gaggle of seven *big* Muscovy ducks, counting the parents. And they thought my dock was "home." They came "home" to roost every night. Soon the piles they left behind — nearly a peck (no pun intended — a peck in volume — every morning!) got to be more than I could handle.

I began shooing them away with an old yellow broom. They didn't seem to get the message.

"Spray insecticide all over the dock," Frieda, the next door neighbor told me. "They don't like the smell."

I did that. The ducks didn't notice. I chased them off with the yellow broom. They came back that night. If I had known what lay before me, I might have considered trucking in a few more alligators to finish off what they started.

The next day I poured a bottle of ammonia all over the dock. Since the fumes burned my eyes and nose, I soaked the boards with the smelly stuff, hoping it would do the same to the ducks. The piles were there in the morning, as usual. I chased them away and cleaned up their mess with my old yellow broom several times a day.

For a week I secretly contemplated using hot sauce to drive them away, but my conscience wouldn't allow it. One day the piles of smelly stuff were almost too much to move. Finally, I put the *hottest* sauce from my cupboard in granola. When I saw them all together on the dock, I took it to them personally to be sure other birds would not get the fiery banquet. The seven Muscovies waited eagerly as I spread the mixture on the deck before them. Broken-hearted at my own cruelty, I turned my back to run toward the house. Looking behind me in shame, I saw all seven diving into the treat. They ate every last speck *–quacked* — and looked around for more! Since I wasn't serving anything else, I banished them with my yellow broom.

"Hook up the hose so you can blast them out," advised a friend. So I rigged the hose with the "jet" power spray aimed directly where they roosted. At 7 p.m. they were all "home" so I ran out, turned on the water full-blast and waited for them to scatter. They loved it. Ducks love water, even when it comes at them sideways! I almost got the father duck with the yellow broom that time.

Those ducks walked or flew or swam wherever they wanted to around my property, so I decided they might be discouraged if I put up a barrier to the little "bridge" that goes from the lawn to the dock. I should have known it wouldn't work; they just flew over it. Then, I reasoned, if they are in the water and contemplating getting on the decking, maybe if I put barriers around the dock that they can't see over, this would keep them off. I dragged in huge pieces of rough, broken cement blocks, set them upright all around the platform, which is probably 10-12 feet square. That night they came early. They didn't notice the wall my bloodied hands erected. I employed my old yellow broom, yet again.

Wasp spray, I thought. *It comes out of the spray can in a long lethal stream. I can reach them with that. They can't stand it!*

That night in the dark, I could hear the spray bouncing off their feathers, so I know I hit the target. They sat tight on the railing — didn't budge. They waited while I retrieved my usual weapon. The yellow broom got rid of them for the night, but I had to stand there — in the moonlight — threatening them from the dock, while they finally swam out of sight. (I felt bad, wondering if they could find another place to sleep so late.)

Back in my garage I looked for something, anything, that would get rid of them forever. All I found was a spray can of red paint. By that time I didn't care *what* happened to those darned ducks; this was WAR! I practiced with the paint and found how close I would have to get to hit them. Then I waited About sundown they were lined up across the railing. I crept out with paint can ready. When I was very close, I sprayed the big father duck, thinking if he left, the others would too. He just sat there and let me spray him until the can was empty. In the meantime the wind reversed, so the red spray paint settled on me!

One day I got the bright idea that they would be repelled if the deck rail was sticky to their feet. Instead, I learned that duct tape, wound wrong side out around the railing, is no longer sticky after meeting the elements. The sticky side deteriorated after the rain that night, or maybe it was from the sun the next morning; nevertheless, it was "get out the old yellow broom time" again. It must have been "duck tape." Two of the ducks sat *on* the "sticky" tape and easily flew away when "Old Yeller" threatened them. The tape was, by then, stiff and dry. The piles on the dock were also stiff and dry.

I called the Conservation Department, then the Humane Society: nothing. I called the Fish and Wildlife Division to come get them. They couldn't, but they suggested putting an ad in the paper; maybe someone would like the ducks for supper. I called the Florida Game Commission and the Animal Control people, too. They had nothing to advise.

The ducks roosted in the daytime too and would wait until I could almost whack them with my yellow broom before they jumped into the water or flew across the canal to the other side. It got to be an obsession. I spent a lot of time on my porch now, checking duck traffic. Every morning it was necessary to take the yellow broom to push, sweep and scrub the stinking piles off the dock. I became angrier and began plotting to think of something that would finally do them in. I didn't care anymore! None of my neighbors had pellet guns to scare them away; and I wouldn't let them shoot the ducks with a real gun. Finally, loosing all sentiment, I contemplated *murder*!

One late afternoon, just before dusk, I saw three of them on the dock and lit out after them with my yellow broom, scattering them in the water. They didn't even seem perturbed! My neighbor was on her porch reading the paper and we laughed (well, she laughed, I didn't) about how they still considered my dock their home.

"Frieda," I explained, "I just have to keep at it to change their way of thinking; make it so uncomfortable that they will look for someplace else to call home." The three ducks headed toward my shoreline. They were swimming close together, aligned in straight-across formation. Wickedly, I thought, *"Maybe I can get all three with one whack if I can get to them before they split up. I'd love to — YES! — bash their brains out!"*

So I raised the terrible old yellow broom. Running off the dock toward them I forgot about the cement blocks, tripped on the barrier I had set up for the ducks and fell flat on my face — almost falling in the water where I had just swept the disgusting piles of abominable waste. The broom sailed out and landed on the lawn. The sudden fall knocked the breath out of me. Winded, I couldn't talk and I couldn't get up. My neighbor ran to help. I couldn't use my left hand to help myself stand. With Frieda's assistance, I regained my feet. Recovering composure, I limped into the house and wrapped my swelling wrist in an ACE bandage.

The next morning my shins were brightly bruised, my hand was swollen, huge. An X-ray revealed a bad break in the wrist; they put a cast on it, later a metal-rod support, then physical therapy at the clinic three times a week . . . four weeks . . . !

Now I believe I have just about succeeded — with my yellow broom — in changing the behavior of the Muscovy ducks. They don't come by much any more. I am ready for them if they come! I bought a canister of pepper spray. The next time they visit — if the wind is in the right direction — I'll settle this once and for all!

~ ~ ~ ~ ~ ~ ~

Soon after recording this account, the drake came back. His eyes beaming like a used car salesman, he wandered across my lawn. With pepper spray in hand, I crept toward him, hiding behind a palmetto until he was close. The directions said at ten feet a target could be hit effectively; I was six to seven feet away. Carefully I aimed at his body. I heard the spray bounce off his feathers and was encouraged. I moved the can slightly toward his head. Still smiling, he looked at the stream of poison and waited until it was gone. Then he slowly turned from me, casually looking for better pastures.

Animal rights people will not be sympathetic to this tale, but none of them came with their brooms and shovels to help me. Even the conservationists "ducked" the issue. It's true, I created this problem myself, feeding the mother duck in the first place. I deserved their harassment.

Finally, I realize now, I am defeated. I retired my old yellow broom — stuck its handle in the sand, hung out a white flag and called the moving van. The ducks won the war and I bought a second-floor condo in another town.

Witch Balls, Watch Balls and Watch Bottles, Protecting Early America

by Belva Green

Across a window wall in my home hang ten blown glass balls, two blue, a purple, a green and a red, two yellow, a clear glass ball with blue spots all from the north New Jersey coast, a blue one from Turkey with white eye of God symbols applied around the outside and a smaller silvered ball from Penzance in Cornwall. They hang from lines poked into holes in the tops.

"Japanese glass fishermen's floats," you say? No. One is called a watch bottle, nine are witch balls.

Blown glass spheres known as witch balls were possibly preceded by the colored glass fishermen's floats. In various colors and sizes, hollow blown glass orbs held fish nets afloat until their bouncing signalled the nets were full and ready to be hauled in. At one time both types of balls served a more dramatic purpose.

Early Scottish and English fisherfolk etched their family name, home port and perhaps a scriptural text on a glass float and hung it in their boat. A similar ball hung in the window of the fisherman's cottage. If disaster befell the crew at sea, this float eventually washed on shore. In those days, the beached glass ball may have been the first or only courier carrying the sad news of the tragedy back home. As families watched for the boats to return, these adapted fishermen's floats came to be known as watch balls.

The story is told around Sennen Cove in Cornwall of Ewen Morgan, a young Cornish fisherman. Early in the 1700's Ewen acquired a new bride and his own fishing boat at about the same time. At the wedding celebration the young couple was gifted with a pair of blown glass watch balls. A bit larger than a cricket ball, with a slight greenish cast, they sparkled like the sea, itself. Ewen's bride, Moira Trecarrel, was delighted with the thoughtful presents and took them to the engraver to be suitably etched. Relatives, pleased the couple could start their life together with these traditional watch balls, fingered the inscription:

Ewen Morgan,
Sennen Cove, Cornwall.
God's blessing.

To snugly fit each of the balls, Ewen fashioned a strong cord into small nets, similar to the fishing nets on his boat. In gay spirit, the couple ceremoniously hung one of them in the window of their cottage near Moira's cook stove. She promised Ewen to watch it faithfully whenever he was at sea. Ewen hung the other ball in its net in the prow of his boat, the *Meara Mavelle.*

It is said Moira blushed as she helped him hang the sphere. "I wanted so much to add me own blessing, but for lack of a thrupence. . ."

"Moira, me darlin'," Ewen boasted, "not to worry. Our smack is as seaworthy as any ye'll find afloat."

Brian Morgan, Ewen's brother, commented, "Sure'n but if it be th' yer ship, tis ever beached or the ball is lost, Moira's 'graving could wear away rollin' in the sand and bashed about by waves. Not a worry now, Moira!" Laughing, and perhaps buoyed by the ale of the wedding celebration, Brian carved the name of the ship deep into its bow with his pocket knife.

"And ye know, me darlin'," Ewen assured her, "me and the crew know where there's every jagged rock or boulder along this Cornish coast. Noel Mitford's smack is in the harbor now unloading a full hold at the quay, sayin' they sited a school of pilchard around Lizard Point. We'll be castin' away to get us there right off."

Shortly thereafter the *Meara Mavelle* set upon her maiden voyage, with a new crew and good nets. Moira, like the other Cornish fishermen's wives, aware there were more shipwrecks along the cliffs lining their coast than anyplace else in the world, paced along the bluffs, scanning the waters several times a day.

In record time, with a full live box, the *Meara Mavelle* was just pulling anchor to return home when a sudden storm overwhelmed the crew, ripping the sails, toppling the mast and dashing the helpless wreck toward the 180' high cliffs around Lizard Point. Cold, angry waves rolled over them all. From that day not one was seen again alive or dead.

It was two months before Douglass Murdoch, skipper

of the sloop *Mor Murdoch* out of Newlyn, discovered the floating timbers of the bow, the lid of the live box and the broken foam-flecked mast. When he rescued the watch ball, found silently rolling back and forth at the mercy of the frothy waves, he said the prayer of all fishermen and hung the sphere beside his own watch ball on the *Mor Murdoch.*

It was a fortnight before they made port, some say it was at St. Just, not far from the Sennen Cove settlement. Local people identified the *Meara Mavelle* from Ewen's brother Brian's crude carving. Murdoch set sail for Sennen Cove. Finding Brian, the two made their way to the Morgans' thatched cottage. With Ewen's watch ball in hand they found Moira tending a row of runner beans in her garden. Douglas, himself, broke the news to the widow.

Moira did not weep, even when she saw the remains of the etching, "God's bless . . ." barely visible.

"Brian," she confided later, "I've known for weeks. The watch ball in me window must have told me. I cleaned it and I polished it faithfully — every day — to keep the evil eye from us. One day it started gettin' misty, like a foggy mornin' on the sea. It wouldn't take my polishing cloth; it seemed to dim e'en more. I know now 'twas the evil spirit within it. I watched it faithfully every day, I did, Brian. But I knew — in me heart — that he was gone from me. Brian, the watch ball told me."

In accepting the piece of wreckage and the watch ball, she commented sadly, "And now, I cannot put it away from me lest more misfortune befall us all."

"More's the pity," they say in Cornwall, "but the watch ball done its job."

~~~~~

Crystal ball gazing associated with witchcraft could have originated with superstitious glass blowers They be-
~~~~~

lieved unusual tints or defects revealed in the molten metal to be blown possessed an enchantment that transferred into the balls and could control evil.

Early eighteenth century believers maintained watch balls protected their owner from the evil eye. Hung in the window or from a rafter the shiny ball attracted invading witches already in the home, confusing and distracting them from the treasured contents. Consequently, watch balls became known as witch balls.

The fate of the watch ball could influence a family's sense of security. Their good luck continued as long as the ball remained unblemished. If the ball dimmed or clouded, it predicted a death. If it broke, family well-being was doomed. To keep spirits in check, the balls were faithfully cleaned of dust and soot, polishing away and exorcising evil spirits. So valued were they that they were handed down from generation to generation.

Families used watch balls to cure sickness. If a person or an animal laid ill, the glass ball was immersed in drinking water, a ritual recited and the sufferer given the water to drink. If the person recovered, they believed the watch ball healed.

A watch ball in Elizabethan times, blown with a hole in the top was commandeered to store the family's salt supply. To keep it safe and dry they hung it in the chimney. Salt was expensive then. Should the ball break or be stolen, the family blamed this misfortune on evil spirits, or witches.

Watch balls could be loaned to others following a strict code. The person carrying the ball between houses, under threat of evil, must not speak nor sit while enroute nor may he go inside the new home where the ball would be kept. Further, the transporter must not linger outside his own home after sunset of the day the ball was removed. As long as a ball remained with one family good fortune remained.

History tells us glass houses in England began producing witch balls about 1690. English immigrants brought their customs with them when they settled American colonies. Casper Wistar started the first successful glass house in America in 1739. In Wistarberg, near Salem, Massachusetts he produced blown glass witch balls for sale. It was said there were witches in Salem then, so business must have been good. In 1826, New England glass houses began producing multi-colored witch balls to hang in Cape Cod homes. Heavier witch balls were meant to hang in barns to protect livestock.

The witch balls blown in English glass centers with perky transfer prints inside were not copied in the United States, though a few were made with paper paste-ins for the Philadelphia Centennial of 1876. England and America apparently were not the only devotees to this protection. Details of an entire room are reflected in witch balls in the paintings of many seventeenth century Dutch artists. (Example: look carefully at Jan Vermier's "Allegory of the New Testament.")

Genuine watch balls/witch balls always have a hole in them and should not be confused with fisherman's floats, or the rounded, (heavier) closed balls blown as bowl or jug covers to protect contents from contamination.

Sometimes they are confused with the delicate spheres blown to hold fire extinguishing chemicals or the red-ended red, white and blue balls with plug extensions known as militia balls to plug rifles carried in parades. Plug extensions for glass flagpole finials were similar except they had a knob on the end. Other blown glass orbs included show globes made for pharmacies and darning balls, often oblong, for mending socks. Free-blown balls resembling witch balls produced for supporting rims of vases in shipment from glass factories were so fragile few survive today.

In 16th Century England the witch ball was called a

"watch *bottle*," designed to contain holy water thereby supporting the folk tale relating them to magic associated with watch balls and witch balls. By the end of the 17th century, the watch bottle faded in favor of the witch ball.

Then there is the *witch bottle*! An old Oxford dictionary included witch bottle as ... a stone or glass bottle filled with urine, nails or hair, burned or heated for the purpose of repelling or breaking a witch's power over her victim.

Victorians in America also kept glass balls, often filled with holy water, believing it blessed and protected their homes and families. Since the balls had no flat side on which to set them, they hung in the living room by chain or cord. When the ball was blown, the small hole left in the top was for insertion of a cork or wooden peg and line to hang it. To keep the glass from cutting the line, early glass blowers made a low lip or neck at the top, so it resembled a round bottle. Peddlers sold these bottles at country fairs and door to door. To create more interest and to drum up sales, they corrupted the original "watch bottle" term and called them "witch balls," which more nearly described their use at that time.

Sometimes herbs from the household garden, dill, rosemary, angelica, and the holy ghost plant, all known to be feared by witches, were placed inside the ball through the hole in the top.

Some witch balls have holes both top and bottom, supposedly to let accumulated evil drain away. Colors vary from pure window glass variety to red, green, black (actually olive seen in the light), pastels, patterns of stripes or spots, and the more common blue which, it is said, promises the most protection.

Homes displayed silvered blown glass witch balls in the early 1800's. In 1852, *The Magazine of Art* ran an article proclaiming: "So great is their power of reflection that the entire details of a large apartment are caught up in them in surprising minuteness and clearness of definition and in amusing perspective."

Mirrored glass garden balls sunning on outdoor pedestals may have originated to "reflect away" intruders. Modern mirrored shields used by businesses to protect merchandise from shoplifters are reminiscent and may have originated from those keeping away evil in the past.

Thousands of blown glass target balls were appropriated by itinerant sharp shooters to mesmerize mid-19th Century audiences. These delicate glass spheres were often filled with smoke, feathers or confetti. When hit, the contents were dramatically released into the air. Dynamic performers like Buffalo Bill and Annie Oakley amazed onlookers with their accuracy, shattering ball after ball. Old-timers relate a story that a page rode ahead of Buffalo Bill hurling eleven 2-3" diameter mold-blown glass balls from a sling. As he rode his horse around the ring, Buffalo Bill burst these balls in mid-air with a pistol, rarely missing. They also revealed the secret to his "accuracy." His gun was loaded with shot shells. Shot scatters, so at least one of the pellets broke each fragile ball.

In the mid-1800's the practice of hanging witch balls to protect inhabitants from evil spirits helped American glass houses flourish. The Mount Vernon Glass factory in Oneida Hills made witch balls in blue, green and amber. These hung in barges on the Erie Canal. Samuel Hopkins Adams includes a story referring to witch balls told by his grandfather in his book *Grandfather Stories*, 1989, Syracuse University Press. "To protect themselves from these (evil) powers, the brothers had raised a Pennsylvania hex broom upon the prow of the lead raft and had hung their cabin windows with witch balls, blue, green, and amber . . ."

Still warding off evils, of sorts, the influence of the witch balls continues to bewitch people to this day. Annette O'Connell agreed in a story in the *Old Bottle Magazine*, May, 1986, that most old glass gaffers did not believe in witches, although histories tell us eighteenth century witches were hanged in New England.

"As late as 1968," she wrote, "a 70-year-old New Jersey glass gaffer was asked to make a witch ball. He declined saying 'Good luck don't happen to them who makes witch balls.'"

Belva Green, author of HOW THE ROBIN GOT ITS RED BREAST (Independence Publishing Inc.) writes re-told folk stories, contributes to antique and collector publications, conducts occasional writers workshops for children and adults, and lectures on antiques.

Gone a-Hunting

by Jim Weiss

"I brought baloney and cheese sandwiches. Sit down and take the load off your feet," my father said. A pure, American working class man, he stood a bit over six feet, hair thinning on top. Once powerfully built, time was chipping him away.

As soon as I sat down and began to unwrap the wax paper from my sandwich, following my father's lead, lickety-split a rabbit, all fur and pumping its motor legs broke from a hollow spot at the other end of the log!

Caught off guard, my father stood and fumble-thumbed for that impossible safety. He shot. He missed. By the time he could work that bolt, Br'er Rabbit was long gone. I had witnessed my father and his bungle gun before.

I was twelve then. My arms and legs must have looked as if they were fresh squeezings from a Colgate toothpaste tube. A few inches of snow covered the ground, and Lake Erie's winds bit my face to a blotchy red. We had just worked a friendly farmer's cornfield, and we were in a wooded area that contested the cornfields for living space.

I carried the Stevens single shot, over and under .410, a hand-me-down shotgun, passed on from father to son. My father had a hopeless piece whose make I won't mention. It was a bolt action, of all thingamajigs, 16-gauge, and had a foozle-thumb safety. Anyone from the makers of a good shotgun, like Remington, could have told the folks who had made my father's shotgun that a thumb safety and a bolt action on a shotgun were enough to handicap any hunter; they were bad news and fit only for a cartoon rabbit hunter like Elmer Fudd.

"Saxnote, divine ancestor of the Saxons, this warrior has lost his skills," I unintentionally voiced a thought after witnessing my father miss his shot. (I had been reading a book about our family's ethnic heritage and had some inflated ideas).

"What did you say son?"

"I said it was a tough shot dad. Do ya want ta track it?

Another time, his brother, my uncle, the family's grand huntsman and the master of a real hunting dog, a Weimaraner, had once chuckled and confided, "Jimmy, you know your father hasn't the heart to shoot anything."

Hunters in the Snow

Lake Erie's winds showed no mercy. Northern gusts and flurries worked our exposed trigger fingers until they were as cold as deep freeze ice. Fourteen years later, at age twenty-six, it was opening day on public hunting land, and the gunfire seemed to unintentionally substitute for all of the battles fought in northern Ohio during the War of 1812—there were many of them. (I was still reading history books).

A game bird, trying to fly as fast as a jet, made it skyborne in the bleak distances of the battlefield! Guns up, howitzer angled smoothbores let loose. Slap stinging, spent shot scored hits on our field clothing, exposed hands and faces. We had just formed up—no words spoken, fire teams abreast-to work our own wintered-in patch of land. Now it had become a field of incoming fire.

Satch, our clown, walked to Jake and handed him his 12-gauge, Browning auto banger, meaning that Satch's father had money, above just being a working class man. Bending over and touching his toes, he pointed his wide rump to where the gunfire had sounded.

"Hey Little Steve, why don't you just paste a target on my butt so those guys can get it over with? Yoo-hoo, can you guys hit this?" At two hundred-sixty pounds, his backside presented a large enough target.

Big Jake, the fourth of our gang of the four who usually hunted together, cautioned, "I wouldn't say that too loud if I was you."

One of the traits that I liked about Satch is that as a rookie cop, he could take a hit and come back at the system or the bad guy. A lot of cops just stopped trying to do the job. Satch wasn't a quitter.

As if in response to Jake's words, a pellet-flinging cannonade sounded for the fourth and final time. Other hunters' spent shot rained down on us, unintentionally of course. After being frozen to our bones; "temporarily" lost in the woods once; the only bird shot had been the hen pheasant that I bagged with the .410.

Little Steve usually possessed the patience of his Russian peasant ancestors, and now he spoke what all of us felt. "Well, I don't know about youse guys, but that about does it for me." A gust of Lake Erie's bone chilling wind, with snow on its breath, reinforced his words. "There has to be a better way to go hunt'n."

Plans for this big hunt had finalized days before. Jake and I were gung-ho cops back then; we'd been in the police department a few years, but we were still young. Satch, the other hand, had been the only one of us not to follow a fist-hard, Northern Ohio working class tradition—military service. Maybe that's why his shooting reactions tended to be slow. Jake, Little Steve and I would have thought of ourselves as shirkers if we hadn't volunteered for the army or marines right out of high school. Likewise, we would now have thought less of ourselves if we hadn't gotten up extra early on opening day and gone hunting. Our fathers and uncles had all gone through this stage.

So that none of us three cops would appear too bossy, we, following an unspoken rule, gave the green light for our little firefighter Steve to be in charge. This understanding hinged on one of those competitive multifaceted situations, police department politics and all. Even if you've never been a cop, you might know how it is.

Little Steve had kicked us all off for an opening bunny and pheasant season day hunt with, "Let's go hunt'n."

"Where we goin' ta hunt?"

"You know any farmers?"

"I don't know no farmers."

"Then I guess we take our chances on public hunt'n land," Little Steve concluded. No one had a better idea.

"I hate hunt'n farm-raised birds," Jake, with his Tennessee Indian blood our only real hunter, let on. By day two of hunting season, all the pheasants on public hunting land would be harvested out, along with one or two shot hunters. Shooting farm-raised birds was almost unsporting to purists, such as even Big Jake. Their crafty, wild pheasant cousins were nearly impossible to hit, unless you're really good.

Little Steve had befriended us newly minted cops. The way we heard it, the older firefighters at his fire station house were quick to razz him over this. "So, you're buddy-buddy with the cops, are you?"

We would all be the first to admit how lucky we were to land civil service jobs. Northern Ohio's industrial-urban sprawl had another option: become worn-out-before-our-times, steel mill or auto foundry stiffs like our hard times, World War II veteran fathers.

Ours were a hodgepodge of Levi, fatigue, and military

field jackets, complete with proud divisional patches. This mix attracted every thorn and bramble in public hunting land. As a result of being empty pocket guys, our hunting clothes weren't water proof like our middle class betters, like Satch's. Our boots were soaker prone, army combat or Vietnam jungle types.

In contrast to my peewee .410, Little Steve, Jake, and Satch all lugged multi-shot, ack ack throwing, twelves, hand-me-down-from-father-to-son, or borrowed. These were top gun brands: Browning, Remington, or Ithaca.

They were newlyweds yet. He called her "feisty." That first day, after being splashed with a fourth round of spent shot, Little Steve continued, "Besides, I promised my wife I would be home in time for shopping," his wife being the not too humble and at most times a formidable spouse. Well, not that formidable, they had two little ones. It wasn't a secret that Little Stevie would be in for some ballistics of a different sort then what had just rained down upon us, if togetherness shopping were missed.

"Let's get out of here."

"Yeah, my Tizzy has plans, too," second echoed Satch, his mind portraying possible discord on his own home front. Being tardy for a Tizzy undertaking was an unsettling thought. If she didn't get street loads of attention, there could be a mix-it-up. In the overall picture, who cared? Tizzy was every man's dream to look at, a packaged head-turner: startlingly attractive, athletic, legs, blue, bedroom eyed and blond. We were all a little in love with Tizzy. She could twist us around her little finger and embrace us with a glance, the very way that such pretty nurses can.

"Get Gangster Wagon's trunk open," Tovarish Steve encouraged me when my key-fumbling cold fingers wouldn't work. "Gangster Wagon" is what post war Germans named our too-long American cars. I'd heard the Teutons call our American cars this during my tour in their land. This "Gangster Wagon", a '63, foundry-dusted, rocker-panel-rusted, black, low and mean Impala convertible, was mine. All working class boys from our industrial dust-powdered neighborhoods piloted the cars our fathers built, Chevys and Fords, hot numbers, the type of cars a lot of people get crazy in while they howl at the moon.

"I got up five-thirty for this?" someone mumbled. Flesh cutter winds knifed through Gangster Wagon's miserable ragtop and bit into us as if a canvas top couldn't hold off rain or the snow flake piranhas either.

"Firefighters and rookies in the back." Jake set the true pecking order.

"Check it out! Pheasant at three o'clock. Stop the car. Come on, let's go,"

Satch, with his maniacal id and no rookies' paranoia, took charge. Behind me, he moved his Neanderthal shoulders forward, yahooed and slapped the backrest repeatedly.

"Well, it's not fenced or posted..."

What explained Satch's absence of rookie paranoia? He had the advantage of being the favorite and only nephew of a childless record room sergeant. Another uncle happened to be a big name politician.

I pulled off the road to do Satch's persuasive "revenge on the birds" bidding.

In the trunk, across the gun-case-protected cannons lay my bare .410. Satch didn't bother with his and just pounded on the car's rear fender.

"Come on Jim, guns up. I'll bird dog it for you," he said.

"We'll work to the right," Little Steve made to reassert command over the upstart.

We took on a surrealistic quality, dark drab figures on a white background, like the Pieter Bruegel canvas "The Hunters in the Snow." Satch flapped his arms, rushed and then flushed our gun-weary cock pheasant.

Dare I miss? The shot was mine. Was God's feathered creation considering his existence?

I shot a single .410 bang from the classic guns-up hunter's stance. The wildfowl came down, deader than Cock Robin. For the moment, nothing else mattered to me.

Lake Erie's wind-driven snow clouds opened their bomb bay doors, the only way it's done in Northern Ohio. Gangster Wagon's homebound progress slowed to the pace of a snow snail. To go one mile faster would have been like dropping a marble on a linoleum floor—we would have ended up in some field or a drainage ditch. Both Little Steve and Satch became sullen and crowned with gloom at what was to come from their wives.

"Where the blazes you been? We had plans for three hours ago, Satch. Do you remember?" His wife Tizzy's hair-trigger dander was up and she be-bopped about in agitation. She got like this when she wasn't given full time attention. When she had given Satch her orders for the day, she expected him to march to them or die, French Foreign Legion style. She stopped her Satch attack with, "Oh, Hello Jake, Jim and Little Steve." Then more broadsides unloaded Satch's way.

Satch raised both hands in the "don't shoot" position. "But we got caught in a blizzard."

The plain rest of the truth is that he didn't go hunting for the rest of that season.

"Grounded," Jake guessed. "It just must be her day to be crabby."

"Giving full time and attention to Tizzy wouldn't be such a bad deal, come to think of it," I added.

Satch later said of the incident, "I haven't been that embarrassed since Sister Mary Magdalene caught me with a *Playboy*."

Broad-hipped, the wife of Little Steve, met us in the driveway crazily furious, with her face all screwed up and arms folded against the cold.

"Stevie, you promised! Where have you been? Shopping. Remember? Jake and Jim can come in, but not you." On and on her temper skyrocketed. Jake and I backpedaled our way to the Gangster Wagon, and her tongue-lashing continued as wild drama, better not witnessed.

Road bound again, for the last drop off, Jake made a comment concerning the two incidents we had just witnessed. "Jim, you have my permission to kick my butt, if I ever marry." Before the year was out, we both took brides.

A Last Supper

Red brick and full past any days of glory, my apartment building saw itself surrounded by Ford engine foundry hauling railroad tracks, two Ford engine plants, a freeway, an interstate, and an international airport. It had that working class flavor: hear-through-thin interior walls, roach brown carpeting, and pseudo something furnished furniture, turquoise colored stuff that matched the stove and refrigerator, all so groaningly monochromatic.

Older than me by a few years, she was a smallish, unstylish and soft woman, a librarian, whose apartment nested down the hall. Her master's degree in Dewey decimaling came from Case Western Reserve University. She wore rhinestone cluttered frame glasses. She felt pressure. Her only sister and all of her sorority sisters had married, some twice. I knew she would be accommodating. To ask her to a pheasant dinner wouldn't require much bravado.

"Hey, I went hunting and shot some pheasants. Would you like to stop by for dinner?"

She smiled as bright as diamonds but with no common sense, or she would have declined. Her answer was in Baahston tongue, a language form that somehow Ohio's university-educated girls learned to talk when it was appropriate to impress people. Perhaps it was one of those 101 courses.

"Why Jim, I would love to."

Mom had handed me down a Betty Crocker cookbook. There weren't any how-to-cook-pheasant recipes, but there was one for chicken cacciatore. What a tasty, culinary concept pheasant cacciatore was going to be, I thought with self-assurance, and set my mind for a get-better-acquainted dinner.

Hey, it wasn't my plan to send any suggestive messages. Those lights were down low because a couple of bulbs burnt out.

When my mom wanted to do something nice for family and friends on holidays like Christmas or Easter, she would serve Mogen David, the Ohio version of working class excellence. Therefore, my good times were going to roll with Mogen David's finest concord screw top plonk, just a tad sweet with a fruity flavor. Does one dare serve Mad Dog to a Case Western Reserve University alumna? I needed to improve my people skills.

She arrived on schedule and brightly laughed at my corny jokes. The signs, a full moon and all, were favorable.

"Are those peas Del Monte from the can?" she asked.

She spoke Bostonian. Disaster doomed on me at her first bite, and the situation went down hill thereafter.

It was the fault of that first fork load of cacciatore camouflaged pheasant. There was a loud crunching, tooth cracking sound. Something in there broke! Her mouth opened and I swear some little pheasant feathers fluttered out, like Sylvester The Cat being caught eating Tweety Bird. Apparently, one has to dig in and pry pellets, feathers and things out, like Doctor Kildare, when cleaning a shot-gunned bird; I hadn't been that thorough.

Her words weren't Bostonian, but deep-rooted, working class.

"Jiiim, did you clean all of them damned shotgun pellets out?" she said and then recovered, ever accommodating and on a manhunt.

She held her own, exploring and eating tomato and green pepper mucked pheasant in small bites. There were not any seconds, as she moved on to the wine tasting experience.

She went home early, while muttering something about a dentist's appointment.

The librarian and I never quite made it after that, but a year later I married, and my bride was a hot stuff of Sicilian blood. We lived in another apartment complex near my first place. She didn't know squat about hunting.

One Shot Among the Tombstones

"Hey Jim, I made a farmer friend. Said it's OK to hunt on his land. Interested?" Little Steve bounced the ball into my court. Little Steve and I had gone over that farmer's field. We banged a lot, but the wild stuff, mostly quail, was safe from the likes of us.

Steve worked well off to the right. I pointed what was going down, "In front of me, heading towards that old cemetery... a cock pheasant."

My bird, ever threatened, maneuvered to get away among old stones, most dating to the early 1800s. It was one of those tombstone special moments. Looking for escape and evasion, my prey would peek and duck back behind a stone, peek and duck. Was this a shooting gallery or a Saturday morning cartoon? I honestly believed that if I shot before the bird was airborne, it would be less sporting. But if that bird only exposed his head to my .410 shot? No pellets to surgically remove later. A tough decision and one that could have been less costly to a lady librarian's damaged tooth.

The Great Toilet Water Duck Hunt

Again, it was a Little Steve idea that triggered the next hunting experience with, "Let's go duck hunting."

What our search for a duck hunting spot dug up first was, "Yes, you can duck hunt on my swamp farm land. $1000 a year gives you the privilege."

On the other hand, a second offer just about knocked the fillings from our teeth.

"It will cost you $3000 to duck hunt on my land."

Does the taxman know this? If Little Steve, Jake and I added up the total cost of our three wives' engagement rings we would have gotten change from $1000.

When that first farmer stated his price, we turned as red-faced as if someone said John Wayne didn't like us. Reconnaissance by Gangster Wagon along western Lake Erie's south shore found a scrub bush-covered island, seventy-five feet by thirty, in Sandusky Bay.

On it stood the remains of a duck blind. We needed to come up with a creative plan. We would master and cross a black swamp near a brick municipal building to get to the island. Organisms of rot, urine, and worse. It was swamp water powerful. One whiff should have been a convincing deterrent. We tucked away any doubts and went to work, all motivation, to be duck hunting right there on opening day.

Obsessively, we begged, borrowed, and pestered up paddles, decoys, duck callers, one tiny unsinkable fiberglass boat less than seven feet long and probably made with yacht owners' children in mind, plus a yellow rubber raft. Little Steve's father even lent me his 12-gauge pump with magnum shells that, just perhaps, had been used to gun down Messerschmitt Bf 109's in his war. Four-thirty in the morning on the big day, Jake, Little Steve, and I loaded the Gangster Wagon, with the boat tied to its trunk top. At that first traffic light it slid forward, just enough to punch out the ragtop's plastic rear window.

Our plan was rock hard sure. This was America, a land of opportunity, even for poor us. Little Steve, wearing his firefighter boots, the only footwear we came up with close to waders, would navigate out. He would rope pull Jake and me out far enough to be able to paddle. It was a real commando operation. (Some people called him Big Jake because he was six feet four and 230 pounds. Likewise, some people called me "Big Jim," for looking like him). Then Little Steve would hop in the boat with Jake and man a paddle. A pull rope connected our fiberglass *Kon Tiki* to the rubber, yellow gawk raft. It was carrying decoys, blunderbusses, a paddle and Yours Truly. In all, the two rafts-boats carried, oh, at least five hundred pounds with Jake and me in them.

Little Steve weighed in at 145 and stood five foot seven. We had faith in his firefighter's capabilities. Jake and I wore jungle and combat boots respectively. Our minds were set to be in that blind by sun up, easy. After an hour and a half, we had advanced one hundred feet in swamp splosh. Both watercrafts were still dragging on the swamp bottom, going nowhere slow. The water seemed to go from a boat bottom, dragging nine inches deep to a foot deep and then back to nine inches deep again.

"You two elephants think you can get out into this muck and lend a hand?" Little Steve had finally ordered.

So then, Jake, mosquitoes, and I were also out pulling and sinking to our knees in swamp juice. Little Steve, normally not a whiner, had shamed Jake and me out into the Black Swamp goop to pull, too. Today's gumbo served bits of gangrene, putrid matter, and mucus looking drool. We sank down into it past our knees in spots. Our boots were soaked with cold water. It has been said winners don't quit, but the sun came up and it was dead-ended, a muck up, hopeless. We could hear swearing off near the shorelines. No duck worth its feathers would come near this circus. Defeated that day, we would be back—very General McArthur.

Ashore we made our way to one of Lake Erie's last commercial fishermen and his block hut. He hosed the three of us down, laughing so hard that he could not get enough.

"Looks like you old boys been in the sewage muck run off Poop Swamp. That there waste treatment plant is known to cheat a little."

It was a tradition to stop for a beer and eats after hunting. "Black Swamp Bar and Grill" read the sign over a low, cement-block establishment. A "Beer and Food " sign was in the one never-seen-Windex window. We should have traveled further from our folly in the swamp scene.

We walked in to hear from a real duck hunter, a truly nasty character, with a swearword-limited vocabulary and a face as alcohol red as if he were sitting on a hot stove.

"Did you hear those three blankity-blank assholes out in the blankity-blank waste runoff swamp? Those assholes scared every blankity-blank duck to Canada," his mouth ragged.

It was Jake who stated, in a switched down low voice, "OK Jim, if we don't get out of here we'll end up on the chief's carpet. We're about to get pushed into a fight."

Perhaps it was Jake's sure flat face, or it could have been his menacing Indian eyes, or that seen-action field jacket with its "Back from 'Nam" and airborne patches, that stopped the bar talk of the local boys.

"Just could be... Naw, these ain't the assholes." An old, young man wearing muddy combat boots and a mix of field and flannel laid an iron hand on The BigMouth's arm.

Another man in The BigMouth's company looked of age to have been in the Second World War, and he said something, apparently calming or warning, into The BigMouth's ear. By looks, these folks shared our common stock. Did they still hear those muffled drums beat? Do they still?

Never really taking my eyes of The BigMouth, I placed our order with the looks-like-he-came-in-last-place-at-everything barman. "We'll have three of those ready wrapped baloney and cheeses with Cokes to go."

Better, Count Those Decoys Again

Only Little Steve and I made it for that second and last great duck hunt. Erie-dreary pitch dark, and well before restaurants opened, we made it to our Sandusky Bay spot. Ever the Wiley Coyotes, we were going out to the same Duck Blind Island, but with different battle plan. We figured to take a tributary or swash channel in the fiberglass kid's boat, row around a bit of marsh peninsula, and double back to the island. We would tow our gear, decoys and artillery along in the yellow rubber raft. What could go wrong?

Nothing can get colder than Lake Erie's winter. Right off the bat, the shore stood icebound, with a thin you-can-bust-it-up layer of crust going out a couple hundred feet. Breaking ice makes sounds that people can hear for miles when it's smacked with paddles. Lights went on in shore cottages. A door opened, and a man's woken-up-in-rage voice screamed, "You blankity-blank assholes!"

Thinking back through the haze of time, I don't know or can even imagine how we did it. "No one defeats Lake Erie," people say.

We even got our decoys out, boat-rafts beached, and blind set up. Hours went by. Erie kicked up its pitch more. My imagination came and went in fantasy bouts. In the daydream, we were World War II New Guinea-based coast watchers. "Yes sir, you can count on us. We'll let those marines on Guadacanal know if any Mitsubishi fighter planes head their way."

The African Grey Parrot has the intelligence of a five-year-old, some expert has written. How smart can American ducks be? Must be swift, none flew over.

Lake Erie kicked up more. Whoa, something was not right. We put out fourteen decoys. One... Two... Now there were fifteen. What the... Fifteen? Recount. One was not a decoy then. That decoy just paddled.

Little Steve still stared skyward looking for his own Mitsubishis. Lake Erie took to showing its whitecaps. Keep on an even keel and pull this off before Little Steve knows what's up, I schemed.

"Yahoo, scat," I yelled loud enough to impair hearing or at least wake those Johnson Island Confederate Cemetery war dead across the bay on Johnson Island.

"What the..." got off Little Steve.

Daffy Duck's wing tips splashed surface on his up-from-the-water flight. It was a kill shot.

"Where did you see him?"

“Swimming with the decoys. Didn’t you notice?” I stated the obvious to grump him, just a little. Water broke over the fiberglass bow. One duck retrieved, barely. Lake Erie got seriously rough.

“Steve, if we’re going to get, we better be gone.”

How we just barely scooped up our borrowed decoys, I’ll never know. Those last two were almost impossible — Lake Erie doesn’t give up its dead.

Both the rubber raft and fiberglass one were filled with gear and both of us were soaking in cubic inches of freeze-blasted water. Paddle-for-lifers, guns, and all else became drenched. That icy breath north wind washed us up on shore more than our paddling efforts did.

Back at the asphalt lot of the apartment, my wife met Gangster Wagon. Her face screwed up, ever so pre-bubbly, until she caught a glimpse into the trunk.

“If you think I’m cleaning them,” she got out in a spitfire voice, “you’re crazy!” She said this looking at decoys. It needed sorting out.

After the Last Roll Call

Life events overtook us, and those gone-a-hunting days ended. A car cut off big Jake in a police car, red light and siren running, a car with a mom and kids.

His choice was snap fast, but was there really one? He buried Cruiser 202 into the side of a Minnehaha Spring Water truck. Both Cruiser 202 and his knees folded up as if they were Reynolds Wrap-quality aluminum foil around leftovers. Operations and their pain never were successful.

“Well Jim, I imagine it’s a big world out there away from the department. Guess it’s time to go see some more of it.”

Gone a-Hunting

His final handshake was firm, with iron in it. He walked away pointed towards the Volunteer State. He said this at age thirty, medical pension papers in hand.

Three armed robbers, with souls as cold as the devil's, had just shot an innocent man and then got a jump-start on Satch. He hadn't a clue about what he was up against. He was running late to work that night.

"Where's your bullet proof vest?" Tizzy had asked, all concerned.

"Don't have time. Got to run," he said. It would be the worst night ever. He took their first bullet in the chest. It zig-zagged down and around missing all vital organs. Perhaps his huge size saved him, but I'll never know how. He late drew, fired back, and took out the bad guy who had shot him.

Satch never went down, and he won his touch-and-go fight for life. Perhaps Valkyries, those who choose heroes to die, had a change of heart, but the wound caused ruin to a good man in ways left unsaid.

Whatever became of those remaining robbers that night? They fled, tried to hide, and set a guns-up ambush among the tumble downs of the river that burns, the Cuyahoga River. They died by the bullets of their next intended police officer victims, who were smarter and faster than they were. Hell's express delivery trap door opened welcoming their two damned souls.

Satch drew his medical pension while still in his twenties.

She lay stretcher bound, a big 250-pound mound of a woman. Those stairs down had had a hard black corner. A wrong pull, push, lift, or other move, who knew, blew out Little Steve's back. His bad day got worse, a heart attack. At age forty-two, he drew his first medical pension check.

Tizzy, sun-bleached blond and of an unearthly beauty, so billboard American, came to me one August night with, "My itch really needs a scratch. Will you scratch my itch Jim?"

"Tizzy, I think the world of you, but you know I can't scratch that itch." That would be poaching wouldn't it? Clouds covered the stars. A mosquito bit, and I heard a distant thunder. We all make life's choices. Tizzy found doctors enough to play doctor-nurse to that special itch. She ran off with one, but then all of our first line-up of wives kissed us good-bye, back so long ago.

As for me, every now and then, I take that Stevens .410 out from the closet corner for a cleaning, and I think back to those days of gone-a-hunting.

James P. Weiss. Jim served an enlistment in the Army Infantry Reserves and an enlistment in the Regular Army as a military policeman assigned to town/city patrol duties in Germany. His police career included working as a patrolman, sergeant and lieutenant (Platoon Leader) with the Brook Park, Ohio Police Department where he made more than 3,000 non-traffic arrests. He received a BA in Police Studies at Capital University. After retirement, Jim worked as a child abuse investigator for the state of Florida. He freelance writes for police magazines.

The Night of the Little Lanterns

By Louise Bergstrom

Dusk was falling by the time Tamako and Ellie arrived at the gates of Ueno Park. The Tokyo haze had dimmed the early stars, but the garlands of colored lanterns strung around the lake were turning the evening into a fairyland. As they were caught up in the crowds surging through the gateway, Ellie studied the faces of the people surrounding her.

"They look so happy," she said. "I thought this was a festival of the dead."

"Yes, Ellie, it is," Tamako agreed, "but *o-bon* is not a time of sorrow and repentance like the Christian All Soul's Day; it is a happy time, when the spirits of our dead come back to visit us."

"Don't you grieve for your dead?" Ellie asked.

"Of course we do, but during the three days of the festival we must not greet the spirits with sad faces. Instead, we decorate our houses with flowers and prepare their favorite dishes. We have parties with dancing and singing, and we light many lanterns to guide the spirits home."

It was an intriguing concept, Ellie thought, looking down at the small figure beside her. This was the first time they'd been together since they left medical college nearly five years before, but they'd kept in touch. Even though she had lived in the United States since she was a small child, Tamako had surprised her friends by accepting a position in a large hospital in Tokyo.

Tamako regarded her friend with a slight frown of concern. "You have changed, Ellie," she said. "Back in Boston you were always so eager — so alive — ready for anything — but now you are...dimmer, somehow."

Ellie shrugged. "Well, so are you, Tamako," she replied. Although her friend was only twenty-nine, she looked almost middle-aged with her slightly bent shoulders, her pale, round face set in the stern lines of discipline and restraint.

"I know." Tamako made a rueful gesture that seemed to describe the inevitable grinding down processes of time. "We are both older now, and do hard, demanding work. But I don't understand about you and Steve. You seemed so right together. When you were with him, you seemed to be lit by an inner fire — was sure you would soon be married. Then you wrote and said it was all over, but you never explained."

Over. The word echoed through Ellie's weary mind. All the intricate mechanism of a relationship destroyed forever, like a delicate watch smashed on the pavement — like a death.

"It just didn't work out," she said, her voice almost without expression. "Steve got a residency at NOV after our internship and I stayed in Boston. Now I've come here to get away from everything for a little while, and I'd really rather not talk about it."

Yes, she thought bitterly, she had fled halfway around the world only to find that it was not possible to escape from the Beast with its clutching claws that had taken up position under her heart.

Tamako sighed. "Very well, Ellie."

The crowd jostled them briefly apart and again Ellie regarded the happy, excited faces surrounding her. Most of the people wore western attire; only the very old wore kimonos. She felt tall and awkward among all these dainty people who seemed so fragile, yet had survived earthquakes, tidal waves, fires, typhoons, wars, even the ultimate horror of the atom bomb.

Was it ever possible, she wondered, for a foreigner to understand this baffling land whose people were so sensitive to beauty and poetry, yet ruthless and cruel in battle? It all seemed different and strange to her: the language, art, music, attitudes, rituals, their incomprehensible gods...

Swept along by the crowd, they soon reached the little temple of Benzaiten, where a priest was showing colored slides illustrating the tenets of Buddhism. Even though she couldn't understand the words, the slides intrigued her, and she stopped to watch. The children in the audience were stretching up their little hands into the beam of light from the projector to make shadow pictures of rabbits and birds on the screen, but nobody seemed to mind.

"What is he saying?" she asked Tamako when a slide showing a baby resting on a bed of lotus flowers was flashed onto the screen.

"He is saying," Tamako explained, "that although our lives are brief, like waves that break on the shore and disappear, nothing is ever ended. We go on through an endless procession of lives, good or bad, depending on our virtues shown in the preceding life."

"Walt Whitman said something like that in his *Song of Myself*— 'All goes onward and outward, nothing collapses.' Is that what you believe, Tamako?"

"I am not sure what I believe, Ellie," Tamako replied. She looked up at her friend with grave, dark eyes. "Do you remember the Zen garden I took you to see where the stones were arranged so that you could never see all of them from any position? It was meant to represent the Universe, of which we can never hope to grasp the entire meaning."

Ellie nodded. "And it's probably just as well that we can't."

The Beast stirred and tightened its claws around her heart, and she moved blindly on toward the lake. Under the colored lanterns that rimmed it were the miniature night-time markets, hundred of stalls offering their exotic wares: flowers, dwarf trees, goldfish, fortunes, crickets in tiny cages. Several priests were standing near the lake, and Ellie watched an old woman give one of them some coins. In return she received a square paper lantern mounted on a wooden base like a little boat.

The priest printed something on the lantern and lit the candle it contained. Then the woman took it over to place it in the lake, where it floated off to join the hundreds of other little lanterns drifting on the dark water. After watching in silence for a few minutes, Ellie asked, "What do they mean — all those little lanterns?"

"It is part of the *o-ban* celebration," Tamako explained. "On each one is the picture of a lotus flower and some writing that says, 'Funeral services for the myriad of souls of the three worlds.' The priest adds whatever name you ask for, and then you float it off to meet the soul of the one whose name it bears and guide it safely home."

Ellie watched a few minutes longer, then turned to Tamako. "I want one," she said.

Tamako gave her a puzzled glance, then went over to the nearest priest. When she had spoken to him and had given him some coins, he held out a lantern and said something in reply.

Tamako turned back to her companion. "He wants to know what name to write," she said.

Ellie gazed off into the darkness far out on the lake. The name? There was no name. Then from some forgotten corner of her mind it came to her — that favorite name of her childhood that was to have been given to her first-born daughter.

"I will write it myself," she said.

Tamako brought her the lantern, and near the base in tiny letters she printed "Rosemary".

The priest lit the candle, and she carried it over to the edge of the lake to place the strange little boat in the water. It floated slowly away, bobbing slightly on the gentle ripples, streaked with ribbons of colored light from the hanging lanterns above.

"Who is it for, Ellie?" Tamako asked timidly.

"It is for my dead child," Ellie told her. "The baby that I killed." The claws of the Beast dug deeper, and she nearly cried out from the pain.

Tamako gasped and drew back a step. "I—I don't understand," she faltered.

"It wasn't even born," Ellie said slowly. "It was nobody. Nobody at all. Only a few weeks in my body — I don't even know if it was a boy or a girl — but I think it must have been a girl—her name would have been Rosemary. But it was too soon — we weren't ready — we had our internships to finish

— then our residencies — we couldn't —"

She followed the lantern not only with her eyes, but with her entire being as it moved off toward all the other lanterns far out on the lake, traveling into a darkness that was not really darkness at all, but a purifying, all-consuming light at the heart of the Universe; a light that would never go out no matter how fiercely the great winds blew. Lost and frightened little soul — would the lantern find her and carry her safely home?

She felt the Beast loosen its grip, heard it whimper and fall away, leaving only a great and aching void. She continued to gaze across the lake at the cluster of little lights bravely making their way through the darkness to find the souls that awaited them.

"Forgive me, Rosemary," she whispered. "I didn't know..."

As from a far distance she felt the touch of Tamako's hand on her arm and heard her anxious voice say, "Do not follow too far, Ellie — it can be dangerous. Let it go —"

Ellie turned slowly toward her as though awakening from a dream, and said, "I'm all right now, Tamako. Thank you." And together they walked away from the lake toward the glittering lights of the park.

Sleeping Dogs Lie

by Louise Bergstrom

I had barely set down my suitcase before the phone began to ring, and even before I picked it up I knew it meant trouble; I could feel the vibes. And sure enough, there was my niece Susan's frantic voice saying, "Thank God you're home, Aunt Jane — something terrible has happened! Phil's aunt has been murdered, and they think he did it!"

Philip McDonald was Susan's fiancé, an investment broker with a big Seattle firm. A bit stuffy, perhaps, but a totally reliable young man.

"Myra — murdered?" I exclaimed. Somehow the old lady hadn't seemed the type to get herself murdered. "When — and how?"

"About two weeks ago. I would have got in touch with you then, but I didn't know where you were."

"Actually," I said, "I was in Venice. I was supposed to be in Milan, but — never mind. Go on."

"They think she was smothered with that big, flat pillow she kept beside her bed for Maxie to sleep on. There were dog hairs around her nose and mouth." Maxie was Myra's dog — a huge, fat creature of indeterminate breed.

"But why on earth do they suspect Phil? Couldn't it have been an intruder looking for money?"

"No, because all the windows and doors were still locked, and besides, Maxie didn't bark. You know that he always barks at everyone who comes to the door, even people he knows, except for Phil. Mrs. Sheldon would have heard him."

"Mrs. Sheldon?"

"You know, that nosy old woman who lives in the next apartment. She always hears everything, and she was the one who told the sheriff that she'd heard Phil and Myra quarreling that night. Phil and I'd had a date — we went over to Oak Harbor for dinner, and later when he left my apartment, he said he had to stop at his aunt's before going on to the ferry because she'd called and said there was something very important she had to discuss with him."

"What time was she killed?"

"Around 2 a.m. according to the medical examiner."

"But surely Phil would have been off the island by then — doesn't the last ferry leave around midnight?"

Susan lived on Whidbey Island, in Puget Sound a bit north of Seattle. Her apartment was near the hospital in Coupeville where she worked as a lab technician. The apartment complex where Myra had lived for many years was only a few blocks away.

"That's just the trouble," Susan said, her voice breaking. "He didn't leave after all. He was upset after his run-in with Myra, it was late, and anyway, he wanted to have another talk with her in the morning when they'd both had time to cool off. So he went to that motel that's just a short distance down the highway to spend the night, and he called me from there to tell me what had happened."

"Did he say what they had quarreled about?"

"Oh, yes. It seems there's this crazy cult leader who came to the island last spring with some of his cohorts, and they set up headquarters in an old farmhouse near Ebbey's Landing. He calls himself Gabriel and holds meetings every night. Apparently Myra went to some and got hooked. Gabriel told them that Armageddon was just around the corner, and promised to take them to what he called the Place of Safety when the time came — but they had to convert all their assets into cash because they'd need it when they got there."

"Did Myra have very much?"

"Around a quarter of a million in stocks, Phil said. And she wanted to hand it all over to that Gabriel!"

"It's an old scam — hard to believe people still fall for it," I said.

"Well, Myra was getting a bit senile, according to Phil. So when he refused to sell her stocks, she got furious and started yelling at him, saying that it was her money and she had a right to do anything she wanted with it."

"And that's what the neighbor overheard?"

"Yes, and it got worse. Myra threatened to sue if he wouldn't do what she asked, so Phil told her that if she persisted in that nonsense, he'd have her declared incompetent and obtain guardianship. Mrs. Sheldon heard all that, and reported it to the sheriff when they found Myra the next morning.

"Let me get the sequence clear," I said. "After their quarrel Phil left and went to the motel..."

"Yes, and they know Myra was alive then, because Mrs. Sheldon saw her walking Maxie. She went out to talk to her, and Myra told her that she was very upset about the way Phil was acting, and that she was going to take two of her sleeping pills and go to bed. After that Mrs. Sheldon said she didn't hear a thing until around six the next morning when Maxie started to howl. When he didn't stop, she went over to see what was wrong, but Myra didn't answer her bell, so she got the manager with his master key — and there was Myra, dead in her bed, with Maxie howling his poor head off beside her.

"Since all the doors and windows were locked, and Maxie hadn't barked, they think it had to be Phil, who came back during the night and did it. They haven't arrested him yet — I think they're waiting for the final lab results from the pillow — but they've had him in for questioning for hours on end, and he was told to keep himself available."

Great, I thought. Here we had a locked-room mystery and the case of the dog that didn't bark rolled into one: Carr and Conan. "Does he have a lawyer?" I asked.

"Oh, yes, he's got Jake, but there's not much he can do at the moment."

"Don't they have any other suspects?"

"Not that I know of. I'd like to think that screwy cult leader might have done it, but he didn't have a motive. On the contrary, he was expecting to get a nice hunk of money from her. She was just a harmless, slightly senile old woman. Why would anyone want to kill her?" I heard a muffled sob. "Aunt Jane, you've just got to help us!"

"But my dear girl, what on earth can I do?" I asked.

"You can find out what really happened," she cried. "You know, like your Mrs. Anderson always does in your books — spend a night at the scene of the crime to absorb the atmosphere!"

"But, Susan — " I started to protest. Just because I wrote murder mysteries featuring a psychic private investigator, people seemed to think I had the same powers. I didn't, and unlike Jessica Fletcher, who was always stumbling over corpses, I'd never been involved in a real murder case.

"Phil gave me his key," she rushed on. "They're through investigating her apartment, and I volunteered to pack Myra's things — her rent was only paid until the end of the month, and the manager wants her stuff out by then. I've cleaned it and remade the bed—please say you'll come, Aunt Jane!"

I sighed. I'd always tried to be there for her ever since her parents—my brother and his wife—were killed in a plane accident when she was seventeen. "All right, Susan," I said. "Tomorrow — late afternoon. Remember, I just got back from a five weeks' trip to Europe, and I have a few things to tend to around here.

"I know, I know — and thank you, darling! I'll meet you at Myra's apartment — I'll be there all afternoon. I know you're not Mrs. Anderson — but you're awfully clever and I'm counting on you to figure it out!"

Because of the various matters I had to attend to after my absence, and the usual long line of cars waiting at the Mukilteo ferry landing, it was after four before I reached the apartment where Susan was waiting with Maxie. Myra's apartment was in a retirement complex of one-story, garden apartments, built high on a hill overlooking a little harbor.

Maxie barked his usual greeting, and I leaned down to pat him. "Hi there, old boy," I said. I had known Myra slightly through Phil and Susan, and had been there to lunch a few times.

Susan greeted me warmly, but looked rather distraught, and certainly not her usual cheerful self.

"They were going to take him to the pound," she told me, "but I talked them out of it. I'm keeping him for now and I have a friend who'll take him, but you'll need him to recreate the scene of the crime."

"Susan, I hope you realize that this is really crazy," I said. "I'm not in the least psychic, you know."

"I'm not so sure, but anyway there has to be a logical explanation for what happened to Myra, and if anyone can find it, I know you will."

So that was why later that evening I ended up lying in Myra's bed, with Maxie lying sadly — *sans* pillow — on the rug beside it. I lay there going over in my mind all the details I could remember.

What about that man who called himself Gabriel? Surely the sheriff had questioned him — they must have been keeping an eye on him ever since he came to the island. Was it possible that Myra had called him after Phil left that night and told him about the problem she was having with her nephew? Perhaps fearing an investigation into his possibly criminal affairs, he had decided that eliminating Myra might put an end to it.

If Myra had asked him to come over, he wouldn't have needed to break in. But then, how had he locked the door after himself, and why hadn't Maxie barked? No, that theory wouldn't hold water. The manager had a key but no motive, and anyway I knew for a fact that Maxie would have barked vigorously if he had let himself in — I'd heard him do just that once when I'd been there for lunch.

It was no wonder the sheriff suspected Phil; he was the only person who had a key, a motive, and wouldn't be barked at. I suppose the sheriff would figure that Phil was afraid of losing his inheritance, but I knew that Phil was quite incapable of murder and had plenty of money of his own.

Finally I drifted into an uneasy, dream-filled sleep.

Much later I awoke, struggling to breathe. There was something heavy over my face — something soft and *warm* — something alive! I shoved at it with all my strength, and it moved, then dropped to the floor with a thud and a grunt.

When I turned on the light, there stood Maxie, gazing at me reproachfully. I took a deep breath, then let it out in a sigh. So — when the dog got lonely during the night, he would climb into bed with Myra, sometimes accidentally lying over her face, as he had with me. And if she had been too heavily sedated to wake up and push him off...

I reached for the phone on the stand beside the bed; I knew now how Myra had died.

Louise Bergstrom was born in the Cascade Mountains of Washington and spent her childhood in various small towns throughout the Pacific Northwest. Her main ambition has always been to write. Louise completed her first novel at 18 and has been writing them ever since. She has had more than 28 titles published, many in hardcover by Avalon Books and others as original paperbacks.

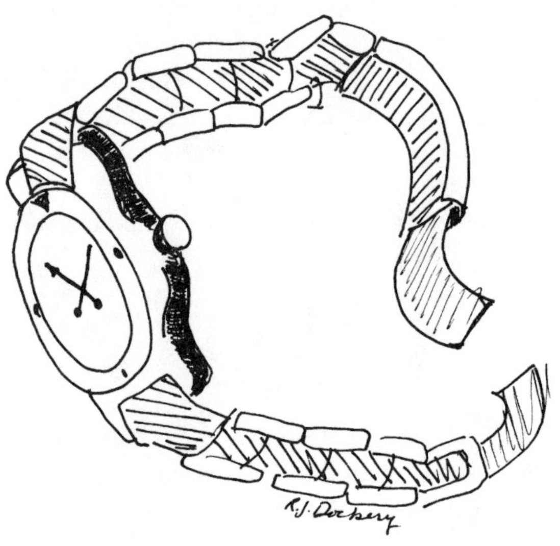

Bumper Skiing

by Robert J. Dockery

"Almost ten. Won't be long now," my friend, Tommy Murphy, said as he looked at his wristwatch, the one his dad had bought him — his lucky charm. He told me how, right after he got it, he had a dream where his dad told him that he couldn't get hurt when he was wearing it. That was last November, two days after his father was killed at the Mill. Tommy couldn't wear it when he was playing football but he would rub that watch before every game, sort of like a lucky rabbit's foot. He'd had a good season and said he owed it all to his dad and to the watch. As important as it was to him, he'd almost lost it a couple times over the past few days because it developed a bad clasp. I told him he should get it fixed before he lost it permanently, and he assured me he would on Monday.

"Maybe we'll be lucky," I suggested as I stood with Tommy in front of Pop's candy store, both of us arrogantly puffing on our Winstons, defying the snow that blew around us and trying to keep warm in our light poplin jackets. The candy store had been closed for hours, and old Pop surely was home in a warm bed, he being much more sensible than two eighth graders. The needle on the big thermometer over the door of the butcher shop across the street told us it was 28 degrees. It always read warmer than the air temperature, even though it was on the north side of the triangular building at the corner where my street linked up with the intersection of Griffin and Cleveland Streets. Everybody called it "Five Points".

The temperature had been dropping slowly since dawn so the storm had begun as cold rain and sleet. The white stuff started coming down in mid-morning and by nightfall the roads were covered and slippery, a sheet of ice dressing the pavement under the new-fallen snow. There were a few tire tracks here and there in the road. Not many people were driving at that time of night in the hazardous road conditions. It would be a long time before the plows and salt spreaders would find their way to the neighborhood, located as it was, far from downtown.

I was proud of my friendship with Tommy who was the most popular kid in my class. We'd been best buddies since the first grade. I was a bookworm and Tommy the consummate athlete, so we made an unlikely pair. He didn't care much for books or studying. Playing sports was his life. He had played different positions on the church football team and was their quarterback for the past two years. He liked baseball too. He played third base last year with the college kids on a team that was sponsored by Hennesy's Bar and Grille. Everyone expected Tommy to start at quarterback as a freshman at Saint Ed's and to take over that position on the Varsity when he was a sophomore. He'd been recruited and would be practicing unofficially over the summer at a camp run by the coach. His dad wanted him to play baseball but Tommy had his heart set on a career in pro football ever since he attended his first Browns game. His dad made sure he got to most of the home games: both football and baseball, to keep his options open. The family even gave up vacations so that Tommy could attend sports camp.

Tommy looked at his lucky watch again. "Hope they

get out a little early. This waiting is getting me."

"Probably will; all this white stuff."

Tommy and I had been to the Canteen at the church and left early to have a couple smokes before the rest of the kids joined us in the cold, snowy streets. We would have hung around in the old cemetery next to the church but that particular night the blowing snow had piled up huge drifts near the rusty iron gate, and we had no galoshes over our leather dress shoes. The weatherman hadn't expected anything like what I saw in front of me, so the Canteen hadn't been called off — the majority of the kids walked anyhow.

We watched as a car come by, its wipers laboring, the blowing flakes covering its tracks almost immediately, leaving a narrow, shallow strip in the powdery snow that glistened white in the light of the street lamp at the corner and, farther down the block, purple-blue in the glow of a full moon. The crisscrossing lines created a design on the road, made more interesting when the cars coming down my street—a long, steep hill — skidded as they attempted to navigate the turn in front of the butcher shop where it takes a sort of switchback and connects with Cleveland Street. Some of the skid marks formed egg-shaped designs.

"You remember what it was like last year?" Tommy asked as he hunched down into his jacket so that his turned-up collar covered his red ears.

"Pretty warm. I remember that much. Not like tonight. We watched from across the street so they wouldn't get any idea about doing it to us."

"Yeah."

Even though my hands were so cold that they were hurting, I made a snowball and threw it after a car as it slipped and slid going up my street. I figured that the driver would never stop to chase us because he would have to back down to the flat part to get traction again if he wanted to make it all the way up to Lorain Street.

"Not many girls tonight," Tommy said. "Made the Canteen sort of dull."

"Most of the girls in our class stayed home because of the snow. No way your heartthrob, Lisa, or any of her friends are going to dance with us with all the older kids there."

"A real bitch."

"Not entirely. The fewer girls the better. And I'd rather have the juniors because they've been around and don't think so much of it. They think we're babies."

"I'd like to be a baby and suck their tits," Tommy said, breaking into a broad grin that lit up his face.

I bent down to make another snowball, slowly packed it hard with the little warmth that remained in my hands and waited for my next victim, already having decided to try to bounce it off the roof of the first car that came along.

Despite the sparse attendance, the Canteen that night elected officers for the coming year. Nobody worried about quorums. It wasn't that formal, and most everyone knew who would be elected well before the elections were ever held.

It was the custom for the kids already in high school to take the trousers off the eighth-grader that was elected the Canteen representative for the freshman class that would begin the following fall. They would toss the pants into a tree so the guy would have to climb the tree to get them while everyone stood around and made fun of him. That dubious honor was to be given to Tommy, another reason for us to have left early. We both figured that there would be no depanting outdoors on such a stormy night and were speculating on what other indignity the upperclassmen might visit on Tommy — and probably me since we were together and known to be buddies.

Tommy and I both were more than able to take care of ourselves and could have given them a good fight. Heck, Tommy was already six feet and weighed close to 200 pounds. But that never happened. It was a sort of ritual that you were expected to endure, one of life's passages that you would tell your children about to let them know you were one of the guys. We could have retreated to my house. I lived two doors up from Pop's. But it would have branded Tommy as a chicken and me as his accomplice in chickenry. Both of us had too much pride to allow that, so we stood in the cold and sucked on our cigarettes and waited for the Canteen to let out at ten o'clock.

"Here they come," Tommy said, and pointed down Griffin. Eddie Mueller and Cappy Jones, two juniors at Ignatius, came out of the Church Hall located at the end of the short block and started toward us. A small but noisy crowd was following along, mostly, I knew, to see how Tommy would take the expected hazing. Cappy disappeared behind a car that moved slowly along the icy road. As the car swung into Cleveland Street with its tires spinning, trying to find a purchase on the slick pavement, Cappy let go of the rear bumper and glided easily to the curb, stopping almost directly in front of us.

"Trying to hide, huh?" he said, looking at Tommy and ignoring me for the moment. Tommy didn't reply. He just puffed on his Winston and stared at Cappy who was about half his size, though three years older. "Wait 'till you see what we got for you and your little friend," Cappy continued. "We're going to test your manhood. Know what that is, your manhood?" Cappy turned, and I knew that he was checking to see whether his gang of sorts had caught up with him. He was the instigator in a group of seven or eight kids who hung around Pop's almost every afternoon and managed to get into trouble regularly with the police. They were all there. Cappy broke out in a forced laugh, like the used car guy on the TV commercial.

Eddie had been elected President of the Canteen and should have been the leader of the hazing party, but he was deferring to Cappy who was the stronger personality.

Tommy took one last drag on the cigarette and flicked it at Cappy who had to jump aside to avoid it hitting him. When Cappy lost his footing on the icy pavement and fell into the snow, the group of about 15 that had now gathered in front of Pop's—almost everyone from the Canteen— laughed spontaneously and even harder than Cappy had laughed. I mentally scored one for Tommy but was uneasy that he had challenged someone who was known as a bully and feared by most of the kids, including me, for his meanness and his volatile temper.

The snowball that I still held in my hand somehow ended up flying at Cappy as he struggled to stand in his leather-soled Cordovans. To this day I don't remember throwing it and think maybe Tommy grabbed it from me and threw it. When my snowball hit him Cappy fell again, this time on his backside. The crowd ate it up, and peals of raucous laughter pierced the crisp stillness of that winter night.

"That's it," Cappy said as he got to his feet. "Both of you guys are in for it now." His gang crowded close to him on either side. I expected a fight and was wondering if some of our friends in the crowd might take sides against Cappy and his thugs if the first punch were thrown. My adrenaline was up by that time, and I no longer felt the cold. All that occupied my mind was which one of Cappy's friends might go after me.

In the silence that followed Cappy's pronouncement, I took the pack of Winstons from my jacket pocket and tapped out the tip of another cigarette, pulled it out the rest of the way with my mouth and stuffed the pack back into my pocket. With the cigarette hanging from my lips, I felt tough enough to take on the world. I lit the cigarette and took a couple defiant puffs. "Let's get on with it," I said, the cigarette clenched in my teeth.

Cappy stepped toward us, and a real row seemed unavoidable until one of the girls shouted, "No fights. Somebody'll calls the cops, and they'll cancel the Canteen."

Others in the group loudly shouted their agreement. "No fights, no fights," they chanted.

"OK, OK," Cappy said. "We'll do the manhood test. Tommy has to hop the bumper of the next car that comes along, and he can't drop off until the car gets all the way to the top of the hill. If he drops off we drop his pants."

There were shouts of support for that test, and Cappy's friends were all smiles. They knew to a man that Tommy had never been willing to hitch a bumper ride and had often called him a coward for not doing it.

"It's either that or the pants — and the shorts," Eddie said, finally taking charge of the situation. "You have two minutes to decide before the girls find out how small you are."

The statement was met with cheers and jeers. One of the girls shouted, "Don't take the ride. We wanna see."

This wasn't at all what I had expected. Even in good weather they never took off everything. They at least left on your undershorts. The girls would see us naked. But Tommy and I had challenged the ritual and could suffer for it. From my point of view I would rather have a good fight than come into my house without any clothes on. We would be the laughing stock of the parish forever. I wasn't dating yet but knew instinctively that every future date I had would come around eventually to reminding me of that night.

"That's dumb and dangerous," Tommy said. "Besides,

even you couldn't hold on all the way to the top of the hill without falling."

Cappy sneered. "Chicken," he said, grabbing the bumper of a Chevy sedan as it passed the Five Points and headed up my street. He crouched down so that the driver wouldn't know he was behind him. People were cheering and pointing but the car continued slowly up the street, its snow chains biting easily into the ice that lay beneath the snow. When the car reached the top of the hill and swung out onto Lorain Street without stopping, Cappy dropped off. Even I felt like cheering when he held both arms aloft before he started back down, sliding a good part of the way as if he were on skis but I kept my hands stuffed in my pockets and wiggled my toes to keep them warm.

When Cappy was about half way down, a white Caddy coming along Griffin Street stopped at the stop sign before it moved slowly through the intersection. Tommy crouched down and ran after it until he could grab hold of the bumper. I thought he would fall flat on his face a couple of times before he got the hang of it and steadied himself. The Caddy didn't have chains and was having trouble, its back end fishtailing as soon as it hit the steepest part of the hill about a third of the way up. Tommy hanging onto the back end didn't help either. Its progress got slower and slower until it stopped. Tommy was still hanging on when it started backing down the hill. He tried to get out of the way, but he couldn't get his footing and slipped under the car when it knocked him down as it slid toward the curb.

After that there was chaos. We all rushed up the hill. The girls were screaming. "Oh, no — Poor Tommy — Is he dead?"

The driver was blowing his horn. Mrs. Piertzkavich was standing on her porch in pajamas. She was shouting, "I called the police. They'll be here right away — who is it?"

Tommy lay face down in the snow, his legs part way under the car and his body wedged between the back wheel and the curb. He was all crumpled up. I could see that one leg was broken. And he wasn't moving or moaning or anything. Cappy wanted to drag him out so we could help him but the driver insisted that we not touch him until the ambulance arrived. The police car was there in no more than three or four minutes. The ambulance arrived about ten minutes later.

I told the policeman Tommy's name and address. He talked to Eddie and then to me. We both told him the same story. We'd been coming from the Canteen and Tommy had decided to bumper ski and the car had stopped and backed down and Tommy slipped trying to get out of the way. He asked the group in general if anyone had seen anything else. Everybody shook their heads and voiced agreement with our story. No one said anything about hazing or about Cappy's dare. The policeman seemed to buy the account and didn't appear suspicious. When the ambulance had gone and the policeman had taken all our names and addresses, I headed home, my head pounding, my hands shaking; my eyes welled with tears.

Right in front of my house I saw one of Tommy's gloves in the snow. I figured it must have fallen out of his pocket when he grabbed onto the car. As I bent over to retrieve the glove I saw something else — Tommy's wristwatch. When I picked it up, I realized that the little pin had come out and the clasp had come apart. The watch was stopped at twelve minutes after ten.

Bob Dockery was born in Cleveland Ohio. He worked with the U. S. Government as a naval architect and later as a mechanical engineer before entering the law. He started writing as a full time endeavor shortly after his retirement from a career as a corporate attorney. He has written over 50 poems, one of which was recently published, and two novels that he hopes to publish. He is presently working on a third. Though he spent most of his adult life in the New York City area, he presently lives full time in Florida with his wife, Sheila.

Jamaican Jolt

by Claudia Sodaro

A nudist island was never mentioned in the vacation brochure. It certainly wasn't part of the plan for Chet and Sally's spring break.

"I am so looking forward to no clocks, bells or deadlines, no 'Mrs. Holtz, Mrs. Holtz' one-hundred times a day and leaving Buffalo, N.Y. to soak up the sun," Sally shared with her husband Chet.

An escape to Jamaica from their jobs as educators in the American public schools, with their daily rules, tools and drools encountered in the classroom, was exactly what they needed.

Couples Hotel, a resort located in Ocho Rios, Jamaica,

catered to newlyweds and couples in love. With his big, brown eyes admiring the blue eyes that had captured him four years ago, Chet knew they qualified for this get-away.

Horseback riding, snorkeling, sailing and fine dining were just some of the activities included in the package. "Let's be sure to climb Dunns River Falls as soon as we register at the desk. I know we've both been looking forward to this after all we've heard about other people's adventures," Chet suggested.

The long flight to Montego Bay and the dusty ride in the non-air-conditioned bus led Chet and Sally to enjoy each other in a refreshing shower enhanced by Castile soap. That scent would capture the wonderful memories they were making, someday. Sally slipped into a crisp, cotton, floral sun dress and heeled sandals. Chet put on a pair of khakis, a tattersall short-sleeved shirt and casual loafers. They surveyed the room with its queen-sized bed, made up with a beautiful, white-eyelet, cotton bedspread.

"Look at the view out this window, the beach, the Olympic-sized pool and the love-struck couples walking hand in hand from the water to their own towels in the sand," she said. "Couples was a good choice on your part, Chet. We'll have to get you one of those shirts with the logo on it. Did you notice it when we were in the lobby? The large lion positioned behind the willing lioness. I can't imagine what they're supposed to be doing."

"After dinner," Chet said in an intimate tone, with his arm around her, "I'll be more than happy do demonstrate what it's all about." They laughed and arrived in the main dining hall. Dozens of tables dressed in their best attire were presented to the approaching two-somes who came from all over the world. The maitre'de sat people with other couples.

"So, you're newlyweds," said Chet, attempting to engage the young couple, who were fawning over each other, in conversation.

"Yes, we're on our honeymoon. We both just recently graduated as engineers and have scheduled interviews when we arrive back in Germany," explained Eric the Red (at least, he resembled a Viking). "You will probably go to the island tomorrow, won't you?" the Reds inquired.

Knowing nothing about the island, Chet always liked to check things out first. "Actually," Chet breathed a sigh of relief after organizing his thoughts, "we have signed up to go out snorkeling at the edge of the reef. Instructions are given at the pool for those of us who have never been."

After lobster bisque, prime rib and key lime pie had satisfied the palates of the couples, they departed. None of them wanted to miss any opportunity to relax and explore this beautiful paradise.

The next morning Sally could barely contain herself. "I've always wanted to snorkel in blue waters like these my whole life! Let's get down to the boat early." Chet loved her enthusiasm. It made every experience twice as much fun.

Couples lined up with gear in hand. What was once plunged in a vat of bleach water would now kiss the lips and embrace the head of some new snorkeler.

The captain of the glass bottom boat explained the procedure. "The spit on your mask will keep it from fogging, and remember to clear your snorkel tube by spitting out any water that happens to enter, especially after you dive deeper than the top level of your equipment. Our three-member crew will be lookouts for you."

At the command, "overboard," couples fell into the water with their attached gear. Chet remained only minutes in the salty sea. As interested as he was in the variety of plant and fish life present, he knew that the "lookout" men were really there to sight sharks. He didn't want to ruin Sally's experience and felt better knowing she had her own personal guard watching out for her — him.

Sally swam immediately to the edge of the reef. The two-hundred-foot drop off was overwhelming and breathtaking. She got a sense of skydiving without risk of the actual fall. The iridescent fish were all part of the picture that beckoned Sally to stay forever in a peaceful world she had never imagined.

It was difficult to leave such euphoria, but Sally knew she must return. No other snorkelers were in sight. "What a beautiful experience; heavenly actually! My throat is parched and sore. I think I overdid it when it comes to spitting water out of the pipe. All my saliva must be totally depleted."

Chet wrapped a towel around her and explained his reason for leaving the water so early. Shocked by his revelation of the shark scare, she thanked him for not telling her. It would have mitigated the peaceful, beautiful encounter.

Back on shore, Chet spotted the sunfish sailboats. Two were left and they were calling to him. "Sally, we've got time before lunch. How about a quick ride?"

An attendant helped them push off and secure their life vests. Chet seemed to have difficulty catching the wind at first, but then he made the right move with the sail and the rudder. The boat took them quickly away from the resort area to view the homes and other spots along the shore.

"The next time we're out, could you show me how to sail this?" she asked. "Perhaps I could catch the wind and get us all the way to Cuba."

"Tomorrow," Chet promised.

Tomorrow came sooner than expected. Like all vacations that are especially enjoyable the time moved faster each day.

The island. It was all they heard about. Yes, there was an island visible from the resort, but Chet and Sally were soon to find out what all the talk was about.

Again, the attendants helped them set sail on the last sunfish available. Sally pleaded to take the rudder. So, she and Chet changed places. At the back of the boat, Sally noticed that the tiller was quite loose.

"Is it normal for the tiller to be that loose, Chet?"

"Not really, but these boats get a lot of rough treatment. So, I'm not surprised."

"I've caught the wind with the sail. Where do you want to go? Cuba, or over to explore the mysterious island everyone seems to be talking about?"

Chet chose the island for starters.

That day, being another perfect day, more couples decorated the beach than all of the other days combined. From the boat, it appeared there was little room left for one additional blanket to be placed.

Gaining speed, Sally and Chet screamed with the excitement of the ride. Taking direction from Chet, Sally operated the rudder and the sail to gain closer access to the island. Not too close to run aground, but close enough to see it.

As Sally began to circle the island, they both noticed a man several feet from shore, standing with a bare backside.

"That man has no clothes on, Chet. Let's get out of here. You take the rudder."

In her hurried state to change places with her husband, Sally nearly fell overboard.

"Sally, are you all right?"

"Chet, get us out of here before that naked man turns around."

The tiller, already loose and quite damaged, broke and fell into the water. Waves took control of the little sailboat and pushed it closer and closer toward the island. People there began to notice that this young couple was experiencing some difficulty. Ten elderly gentlemen began making their way down the slope of the island that led to the shore. At least Sally hoped they were gentlemen, part of the definition of one had always been that he wore appropriate clothing.

While Chet worked on moving the sail and maneuvering what little piece of rudder remained, he noticed a hysterical and red-faced Sally gripping the seat of the boat.

"Chet, have you got it? Have you got it, yet?"

"Have I got what, Sally? There's not much tiller left here to make much of a difference."

"Oh my God, the men are coming closer with their ding dongs swaying in the breeze. Please get us out of here, Chet. Now!"

The "Force", or at least the wind, was with them at that moment, and they were blown sideways along the island and away from the approaching nudes.

Humiliation awaited them everywhere. Hundreds of beach goers stood with hands cupped around their eyes. It made them look like they held binoculars to better view these rookies lost at sea. More and more people, both men and women, came to the shore of the nudist island to view the hapless sailors. Finally, an attendant employed by the hotel swam from one of the stationed boats to offer his assistance.

Sally was so glad when he thrust himself up out of the water because he actually wore a bathing suit. The attendants tied the sunfish to the motorized, aluminum rescue boat and towed the two-in-trouble back to the hotel's shoreline.

After the teasing and hee-haws on the shore, Sally and Chet wanted to retreat to the safety and solitude of their hotel room, never to be seen again.

" How embarrassing!" they whispered to one another.

That evening, hunger forced them to leave their haven. Mortified, Chet and Sally showered, dressed and entered the dining hall. They sat with a middle-aged, English couple, proper, but friendly.

Having made the appropriate introductions, the conversation became quite enjoyable and entertaining. Sally was hopeful that out of their bathing suits, fully clothed and in a totally different environment, they wouldn't be recognized.

At that exact moment, the English gentleman had something he wanted to share with Sally. "You know, Sally, these Americans will try anything. Today, my wife and I saw this young couple out in one of the sailboats. They had no notion of what they were doing, and they had to be rescued."

Sally thought about which one of them knew less about what they were discussing. Was it this gentleman, who obviously didn't know whom he was talking to, or was it she and her husband, who wanted to view a mysterious island?

Oh what the heck, Sally thought, "Those Americans, who will try anything, you see, happen to be my husband and me." The couples had a great laugh, became good friends and always kept their clothes on around each other.

Sally and Chet learned, with a jolt, that when on vacation, it's always advisable to be prepared to enjoy the entertainment because sometimes, unwittingly, one can become part of it .

Claudia Sodaro was an elementary educator for twenty years, wrote for a newspaper for seven years and enjoys both writing stories and composing music.

Night of Anguish

by L.D. Donahue

Andrew Authur McLeary possessed the gift. Be it a blessing or curse, it would be with him always. In cold wrought iron, the words 'My Brother's Keeper' loomed over the insane asylum gate. Beyond the courtyard, in the darkened bowels of the converted medieval fortress, the dealer of death called him "the devil's bastard." A rose blooming in the snow sealed the fate of the young lad who could see the unseen and know the unknown.

Chapter One from the novel THE UNSEEN FACTOR.

The dream remains clear in my mind's eye, even to this day. Drenched from head to toe, a soldier stood at the edge of the swamp. Gold buttons adorned his uniform and several medals hung from his breast. Stubble protruded from his face and a dress military hat sat disheveled on his head. Deep wrinkles of anguish covered his face as he screamed into the pouring rain. Then, with an intoxicated swagger, the soldier descended into the swamp. Mired in the muck, he pulled a pistol from his coat pocket and swung it wildly in all directions.

"Get down! Get down!" he yelled in a fevered pitch. "Enemy on your right flank!" His legs buckled and he dropped to his knees. Slowly, he raised his head toward the rain-soaked sky, placed the barrel under his chin and pulled the trigger.

I stared onto the darkness. Outside my window, thunderous lightning strikes crashed to earth as if the Gods were at war with the world. Between thunderclaps, my father snored lightly, both parents sound asleep in the big bed next to mine.

Silently, I crept up the wall and peered out the window. Luminous flashes, only milliseconds apart, put our front yard in motion. Wide-eyed, my head jerked left and right. Suddenly a white hot vein of lightning struck a giant cypress anchored firmly in the muck some two hundred yards away. The flash brought day to night. A sea of saw grass ebbed and flowed liquid-like before the stand of cypress trees. Darkened figures emerged from the shadows. Startled, I jumped as if a jolt of electricity had run through my body. Thoughts swirled in my head. Was there something there or only sinister shadows playing tricks?

Nose pressed against the window screen, I waited for the next lighting strike. Without warning, a limb from a Loquat tree slapped the screen in front of my face. A scream of terror filled the room as involuntary leg contractions sent my quivering body onto my parents' bed. Like a groundhog, I dug my way between them and shivered uncontrollably until the bed began to shake. The single groan from my father was followed by a heavy snore. Awakened by the commotion, my mother sat up in bed.

"What's the matter Andrew?" she said in a whisper. Arms folded across my chest, I had no reply. Nestled together, we held each other tight until the shivering subsided.

"Feel better?" broke the silence as she combed my hair with her fingers. I gave a nod and she returned me to my bed.

Mourning doves professed their desires in a monotone

chorus when I awoke at daybreak. My parents remained sound asleep as I quietly made my way to the living room. With knees on the bottom cushion, I leaned against the seat back and peered into the morning mist. The aroma of coffee from nearby trailers flowed through the gentle breeze and a wind chime tinkled somewhere in the distance. I placed my chin on my wrist and thought of the dream in the night.

After breakfast, a toot from a 1937 Ford pickup meant another day of carpentry for my father. With lunch bucket in hand and me perched on his shoulders, the three of us walked to the truck.

"Nina!" erupted from inside the cab. "How's it goin' raisin' those two boys?" Then the man let go of a big belly laugh as he slapped the dashboard with both hands.

"Mr. Freck, it's tough keepin' these young lads on the straight and narrow."

"Sister, you got that right!" Mr. Freck agreed.

"Be careful Micky," my mother encouraged, then kissed him on the cheek.

"Come here, woman," my father demanded. "I gotta have more than that!" Still on my father's shoulders, I pushed their heads together.

"OK, OK," Mr. Freck called out. "That's enough, you two love birds. Get in here Micky!"

"Be a good boy and look after your mother today," my father instructed as he lowered me to the ground. Through a plume of blue exhaust, he waved until he was out of sight.

"Andrew," my mother asked, "Would you like to go for a walk in the trailer park?"

Screaming with glee, I splashed through mud puddles in my bare feet as I led the way down the winding limestone drive. The morning was warm and pleasant. Shafts of sunlight flowed through a canopy of live oak and long leaf pine. Along the way, neighborhood children joined in the frolic and when we reached the area of the swamp, I told my playmates about the dream in the night. They believed me without hesitation and we immediately began an excited search. We ran back and forth at the edge of the saw grass and screamed and yelled at the top of our lungs as we peered into the mysterious marsh.

Blanche, my mother's best friend, emerged from her trailer for a visit. They lounged in the front yard on striped canvas beach chairs and chatted while watching us.

"There's a man in the swamp!" Blanche's son, Willie, proclaimed as he ran toward our overseers.

He had interrupted their conversation and, not understanding him completely, Blanche replied "Do what?"

"There's a man down there in that swamp, Momma."

"Who says?" she asked.

"Andrew" he said confidently.

"Andrew Arthur McLeary, come here, please." The wavy musical delivery came from my mother.

I made my way through the herd of children and stood at attention before her. With the group huddled behind me, she asked in a soft voice, "Andrew, do you say there's a man in the swamp?" I nodded.

"And who would this man be?" she continued.

"A soldier," I replied.

"A soldier?" she repeated. I nodded. She paused for a moment, took a deep breath, then let it out slowly. "When did you see this soldier in the swamp?" she asked.

"In my dream last night," I replied. Her eyes lit up and she released a faint laugh of relief.

"Well!" she exclaimed. "He better be careful in that swamp because the alligators are going to get him!" My scream was echoed by the other children as her snapping fingers pinched my body.

One week after my dream, the first sign of death darkened our door. He stared through the screen with bulging black eyes. Thick strings of saliva drooled to the floor. Suddenly, the vile stench rushed into the living room. Gagging violently, my mother and I ran for the back door. Sparkey, our neighbor's dog, had found the rotting corpse.

After a few deep breaths in the backyard, we broke into a round of hysterical laughter. Within seconds, Sparkey's front paws were on the white picket fence that enclosed our back yard and he barked at us incessantly as we rolled in the grass.

"Sparkey, you nasty boy!" came from my mother when our laughter turned to moans. On rubbery legs, we leaned against one another, contemplating our next move.

"Let's run in the back door, out the front door and down to Helen's" Nina whispered. I gave an affirmative nod. With screened doors banging behind us, we ran to the driveway where Sparkey waited.

In an auctioneer's cadence, my mother yelled "Get away, get away, get away, get away, get away," until we reached Helen and Ralph's trailer.

In a white rattan rocking chair, Helen sipped coffee on the front porch as Ralph watered a Cape Honeysuckle bush near the corner of the lot. With Sparkey on our heels, we sought deliverance behind Helen's chair.

In a low masculine voice and startled tone she asked, "What in the world's going on here, Nina?"

"Your dog's been swimmin' in a sewer or something?" Nina replied. At that point Helen got a sniff of Sparkey.

"Ralph, get this dog away from me!"

Running to the porch with garden hose in hand, he asked, "What's the problem?"

"Good gosh man, can't you smell that?" she replied in a tone of disgust.

Ralph grabbed Sparkey's collar and pulled the dog toward himself until their heads almost touched. One breath and Ralph reeled backwards into a pigmy date palm. Screaming from the needle sharp thorns, he rolled onto the thick grass in pain. Sparkey sensed his master's distress and licked Ralph's face.

"Nooooooo," rang out as he rolled across the yard until a car tire flower garden stopped his retreat. Ralph sprang to his feet and ran for the garden hose. "Bring some soap, Helen! This dog's been rollin' in somethin' dead!"

The following Saturday my parent's had planned a shopping spree and I was dropped off at Blanche's trailer for the afternoon.

"Come on in, Andrew. You know you don't have to knock," followed my rap on the screened door. Stretched out on the couch in yellow blouse and white shorts, Blanche held out an arm of welcome and I ran to her embrace.

"Andrew, do you love old Blanche?" Head nodding quickly, I hugged her neck. "I love you too, baby," she whispered while patting me on the butt.

Eager for a match of checkers, William motioned me to take my place at the dinning room table. Black and reds marched across the checkered board until hunger pains brought the contest to a close. Blanche had fallen asleep during our tournament and, seizing the opportunity for a benign bit of mischief, we silently placed pieces of toilet paper, one square long, between her toes.

"Wake up, Mama. Wake up Mama, I'm hungry."

Night of Anguish

Blanche stretched her arms toward the ceiling and groaned. "You boys hungry?"

"We're starvin', starvin', starvin', Mama!"

"Okay then, what do you boys want?"

"Jelly biscuits" we replied.

"You can't live on jelly biscuits!"

"Yes we can, Mama. We want jelly biscuits," Willie pleaded.

"Okay then," she agreed.

Toilet paper between her toes, she walked to the kitchen as we snickered on the couch. William slid onto the floor and we broke into an orgy of laughter.

"You boys are really silly. Silly boys, you really are," came from the kitchen. Unable to keep our trickery a secret any longer, we pointed to her feet. She shook her head and laughed at the ridiculous sight, then danced around the kitchen table, toilet paper wiggling between her toes.

After lunch, William and I immersed ourselves in a game of badminton while Blanche sun bathed. The gentle breeze which had blown from the north for the past two days, abruptly shifted course and with the new flow, came the smell of death from the swamp.

"Lord have mercy on my soul, boys! What in the world is that stinking?" Blanche cried out. We shrugged our shoulders and kept playing. "Willie, come here and smell my feet." He ran to her side and sniffed both feet.

"I don't smell nothin', Mama."

"There's a soldier in the swamp," I blurted out. Sitting up in the blue and white beach chair, she looked at me intensely.

"Andrew, I remember now. You told me last week."

"Why won't you believe me?" I asked in desperation.

"I do," she said, pulling me to her breast. "I do believe

you, Andrew. Come on, boys, Lester will help us."

Lester Noland lived two trailers down in the back corner of the trailer park. He was a hillbilly from Tennessee with a reputation of drinking daily and fighting whenever the mood struck. Rumors in hushed tones said he was a moonshiner who came to Miami to escape prison, but he loved children and I had no fear of asking him for assistance when my pedal tractor slipped a chain. In the shade of a gnarly live oak, he plied his trade as a mechanic, and he always smelled of whisky, after shave lotion and grease.

William and I ran to Mr. Noland's home where we found him working under a big black sedan. The front wheels were on cinder blocks and the hood had been removed. We knew that Mr. Noland never spoke to anyone when he was busy, so we sat cross-legged below the front bumper and watched in silence. A few seconds later, Blanche arrived. She peered into the engine compartment and, like William and me, watched quietly.

Fifteen minutes later, "How can I hep ya?" came from underneath the car.

"Well, uhhhh..." Blanche stammered. "It's kinda weird."

"Talk about weird! Honey, you makin' some kinda fashion' statement with that stuff between your toes?"

"Boys, get that stuff off me!" she commanded. Under the car, smiles and silent laughter passed between the three of us as Willie and I removed the toilet paper from her toes. Mr. Noland crawled from beneath the car and leaned against the front fender.

"Give me that one more time, Blanche."

"Les, uh, Andrew says there's a man in the swamp."

"Is that right? Hmm!" he mused.

"A soldier," I said eagerly.

"And I guess ya'll want me ta go in thar 'n look fer him, don' cha?"

"We'll go with you! We'll help!" William encouraged.

"Now, lookee here, boys. 'Atsa bad place ta be. They's libel ta be snakes out in thar — er... alligators!"

Mr. Noland thought for a few moments as he looked over the landscape. After pondering a large pine tree adjacent to the swamp, he turned to us abruptly, "I'druther have pine resin on my hands than mud on my feet!"

We trailed along behind him to the base of the tree and watched as he climbed to the top. He broke off a couple of small limbs to clear his view and we waited. Within a minute or two, he hurriedly descended. Fifteen feet above the ground, he sat on a large limb to check his breath. "Blanche," he began, then paused.

"Better call the Po-lice."

Without a word, Blanche ran to the trailer park office. Mr. Noland, upon completing his descent, sat on the ground and leaned back against the tree.

"Now, boys, I don't rightly know how ya'll knew 'bout this, but thar's somebody down in thar deader'n a doorknob. 'At's right. Now lissen ta me. I didn't have nuthin' ta do wid it. You boys know that fer sure, don'tcha?" We both nodded. "Jus' leave me outta it, okay?" Again we nodded. He stood up and walked to the yard full of cars, jumped in a '39 Willis coupe, cranked the engine and slammed the door. Like two zombies, we stood motionless.

The car rolled forward and he stuck his head out of the window.

"I'm a get'n the hell outta here afore the shit hits the fan, boys," and drove off.

No more than fifteen minutes had passed when a black and white squad car stopped in front of Blanche's trailer. We stood in the front yard as the officer approached. His mouth hung open and his lower teeth protruded above the lip.

"Mrs. Blanche Sexton?" he asked raising his head from a notebook.

"Yes, sir" she replied. He returned to his notes.

"I understand you believe there's a deceased person in the swamp?"

"Yes, we do."

The wind shifted and the terrible smell returned. After a long whistle, the officer remarked, "Brother! Woooeee, that's bad! That's some stinky stuff, ain't it, boys?"

We both nodded and replied "Uh-huh."

"Mrs. Sexton, I'll put my rubber boots on and see what I can find out for you."

He opened the car trunk, slipped on his boots and ventured off into the saw grass. William and I used his dark blue hat for a beacon as we followed his every movement from the driveway. Suddenly he stopped, then staggered back a few steps.

"Damn!"

He retreated from the swamp like a spooked animal, swinging his arms wildly as he splashed his way out. Speckled with mud, he fell onto the driveway gasping for breath.

"Dead. Somebody's dead," he managed in a labored whisper. "Help me up, boys."

Still out of breath, he staggered to the squad car and grabbed the radio. The request for a detective went out immediately and, after some talk back and forth, a coroner was requested as well.

By the time the detective pulled up in a brand new, solid black 1948 Ford sedan, a sizable crowd had gathered. Near the front of the group, in a mournful voice, a gray-haired woman repeated, "Lord help me!"

My mother and father, back from their shopping spree, joined Blanche on her front porch. The coroner's vehicle arrived a few seconds later and all of the officials huddled at the edge of the swamp. After conversing at length, the police officer led the detective, a coroner, and two assistant's into the swamp. Thirty minutes later, they emerged with a body bag.

As the dead man was being loaded into the coroner's vehicle, the detective stood on the front bumper of his car. Holding a military hat in his hand, he folded back the leather sweat band and asked, "Does anyone know Horace Pittman?"

The gray haired woman fainted.

"It's her son!" someone cried out. "He's a soldier!"

Blanche and my mother looked at each other with lifted eyebrows. From that day forth, an understanding ear would always be turned my way.

L. D. Donahue began his professional life in the entertainment business at seventeen as a percussionist. A published composer and lyricist, his romantic musical comedy 'Staking My Claim' premiered August 17, 2000, at Largo Cultural Center's Tonne Playhouse in Largo, Florida. THE UNSEEN FACTOR is his first novel.

Ageless Compassion

by Mary Beale Wright

Today, thankfully, adults care deeply about children and children's feelings. If a school tragedy occurs, no matter the grade level, counselors go directly to the site, seeing that the children affected receive the help they need to handle this harrowing situation. Or, should a child be having difficulties of some sort, the guidance counselor may refer the child to a more specialized professional. In my day, not so at all: adults too often shoved children out of the way, forced them to keep quiet — "Children should not be seen *or* heard," rephrases the old statement. Children did not have feelings. Who cared?

On Sunday afternoon, January 4, 1931, our mother died suddenly. Home only a day, following a hospital stay and long convalescence, she seemed ready to pick up the threads of her life in southeastern Pennsylvania as a farm wife and a mother of eight children, the last a two-and-a-half-month old girl.

As we older children left to go outside, she was conversing with her teenage nephew and our father was upstairs taking a bath. Six of us, with our oldest brother William leading, went out to enjoy the balmy, spring-like weather, taking a walk in the fields and lower meadow. Along the way we spied a bouncing cottontail, something to tell her about, since she loved bunnies and squirrels, never wanting them to be hurt.

Bubbling with this wonderful news, we came back to chaos. Dumbstruck, we could see our mother lying very still on the couch in the corner, our father hunched over in a kitchen chair by her head. He was crying — the only time I have seen him so. Cousin Kirke, too, was crying and shaking, in a heap by the fireplace across the room.

How Aunt Bess, our father's only sister, had arrived at our place twenty miles from her home, I don't know. Someone — it may have been she — showed us our mother, telling us she had "passed away," was "gone," but no one explained to her bewildered children what those terms meant. We did realize something bad had happened. Then we were shooed upstairs, where we huddled together in our four-poster bed in the room directly above.

From this place, we could hear the scurrying about; the hushed, excited voices; and the strange bumps and knocks. We wondered what was going on.

No one told us we could not look out the windows. From the side window we could see the comings and goings. We saw our mother brought out and slid into the back of a long, black vehicle. Rushing over to the front window, we could see it bump down the rocky lane.

"The hearse," William explained, remaining dry-eyed. (Maybe he dared not cry in front of his younger brothers and sisters; he would have had a lot of company, that is for sure.)

Then our cousin Richard arrived, Uncle Johnny with him. We knew Cousin Richard's big square Chevrolet with the disk wheels, since barely a month before he had driven Mother and the baby, as well as a sister and me, to Atlantic City, New Jersey. There Mother rested, Aunt Bess joining us. Shortly, they led Cousin Kirke, still in shock, to the car and helped him in.

Not long after that, the neighbors from the next farm

arrived. They went into the house, out of our sight. Later, they emerged. The lady, who limped heavily, carried a bundle with great care. The man lugged a cradle.

"Rosalie's," William told us. "That's her blanket." (As it happened, this was the best thing to occur that day. Without a mother's care, she might well have died. She is a grandmother herself now.)

Some things need to go on, no matter what. So it was, on our dairy farm: barn work and milking must be attended to. The three boys left us little girls alone for some time. Meanwhile, it grew dark.

When William returned, he lit the coal oil lamp, relieving the gloom. Seeing us so anxious, he reached for the pile of little books Mother read every night. First, he read Beatrix Potter's "The Tale of Peter Rabbit." Our anxiety began to recede. Although he must have been hurting terribly himself, as the oldest, he must have somehow felt accountable. Putting his own feelings aside, he then chose one of our favorites, with mean tigers aplenty, and began to read this story. We relaxed. Someone giggled.

"What are you children doing?" From the darkness of the upper hall Aunt Bess suddenly emerged. Ordinarily she was not unkind, not as she was this time. She spied William with the book, his little sisters gathered around him. "Close that book immediately!" she ordered. "And all of you be quiet!" She sniffed indignantly. "Your *mother* has just passed away! Noise! At a time like this!"

Poor William. He did not say anything, but did as she said. We could see how upset he was. I know I felt very bad for him.

With that, it grew colder and bleaker. We all snuggled down under the quilts.

The next few days are blanks, although I do remember

the funeral a little bit — when we children were herded past her casket to see her a last time.

Over the years, I have managed to put aside much of what happened that day. But I have not forgotten that our brother, in spite of his own deep hurt, reached out to his younger siblings and comforted them as best he could, his own compassion spreading over them. At the time, William was only twelve-and-a-half.

Mary Beale Wright grew up in southeastern Pennsylvania, the fourth of eight children. She lived in Maryland for 43 years, retiring in 1995 after teaching English on the secondary and college levels. Married, with two grown children, she is also the grandmother of two. She and her husband moved to Florida several years ago.

Clinicals

by Joyce Palmer

Prologue: I have been intrigued by medicine since I was a child. I see hospital staff as such important people for the simple reason that when someone is sick, they have the power and knowledge to make them better. Some of the most profound experiences in my life have come from "Clinicals" which are on-the-job training.

"One, two, three, four, five. Air! One, two, three, four, five. Air!" said the paramedic, with each series of compressions on his unresponsive patient. "She has no shockable rhythm!" he added in loud tone.

"I'll take over compressions!" I said, moving quickly to take his place. I quickly scanned the patient. She was a white female, maybe sixty or seventy years old, with an established IV line, defibrillator leads attached to her torso, and was being given oxygen by an endotracheal tube. My attention became acute. My focus was solely directed at my hands on the patient's chest that were trying to restart her heart. Immediately the paramedic began giving information to the doctor.

"The patient had had open heart surgery about a two

weeks ago. Her daughter said that she had a bad valve as well as arterial blockage....."

I tuned the rest of the conversation out as my eyes quickly examined the scar in the middle of the patient's chest. Between the compressions, the doctor checked several times for shockable rhythms. After many more compressions, the patient was pronounced dead.

My mind took several minutes to adjust to the idea because when my hands had left the patient's chest, her skin still had warmth to it. For a moment there was silence — a very brief one, just long enough for us to ponder the fragility of our life and the incomprehensible selection technique of death.

The paramedic started talking again. Sounds of conversation floated by without my registering what was actually said. I was in daze, feeling as if the death of this patient was somewhat part of my responsibility.

This happened mid-morning, a few hours after I arrived at the hospital as a student doing clinicals for my Emergency Medical Technician (E.M.T) course. I helped to bag the body, and it was during the bagging that I really looked at the patient. Her hair was short with small frizzy curls that were partially gray and partially dyed. Her eyes were grayish green, her thin lips appearing as a small line on her face. Her weight was between thin and pleasingly plump. The health professionals would probably describe her as being within normal body weight for her height. Minutes after we bagged her, her crying family entered the emergency area; they spoke, then swore, and then apologized to the hospital staff.

Despite the fact that this was a tremendous experience in my clinical life, my whole day would probably have passed without my going back over the episode. The day would have been logged as all my other clinical days — date, time and events to be turned into my teacher in my clinical log. However this day was different because the patient's family decided that an autopsy must be performed. Apparently there were some discrepancies among the insurance company, the doctor who performed the operation, and of course, the huge bill that had accrued from the heart operation.

When I told the nurse what I was thinking, she said that I was crazy. She told me I would not be able to eat lunch afterwards, and that it would be the sickest thing that I had ever seen. Then she added that she did not know if they would permit me to see it, even though that it would be a great learning experience in anatomy.

A call was made to the pathologist. I was described as pleasant student who wanted to eventually become a doctor. It was joked that I would be eternally grateful for such a puking experience. I sort of hoped that the pathologist would say no to my request and quote some hospital rules as justification. The thought of lunch was the only deterrent in this whole deal. The hospital had a good lunch menu that day: fish or chicken, mashed potatoes, and choice of salad.

"Joyce, I will have to dress you!" the nurse said as soon as she got off the phone. I sort of felt afraid; her tone and her wink hinted that I was just about to go through hell.

The pathologist turned out to be a woman, short (somehow I had always pictured pathologists as tall men), her square face sporting spectacles and her hair covered by the same anti-contaminating cap that I was wearing. She spoke with a high pitched voice telling me that all that being a doctor involved was money, hard work, time, and commitment. Her assistant, who was also a female, seemed pleasant and she told me not to worry in her effort to put me as ease as this process is similar to dissecting a chicken.

My first impression of the autopsy room was one of discomfort. The room had no windows. It was small with a large stainless steel table in the middle of it that had holes for the water to drain through. In the walls were maybe four refrigerators, with temperature controls on the outside. In a corner of the room were lockers, a sink, tools and containers. Above the metal table a scale hung. On it were piles of towels, and beside the towels was the body of the woman.

At first everything seemed OK. We all began chatting about life's generalities. The pathologist's assistant told us about hunting with her husband and cleaning the deer. I spoke about the patient, about how sad it was to die after going through all the trouble of having an operation. Then whatever ease I had about this whole process dissolved. When the pathologist started cutting the chest region, a bright yellow subcutaneous fat appeared, and I gasped. The flap of skin from the chest region was pulled backwards covering the face of the patient, and the rib cage became apparent. The rib cage was then removed and the organs of the upper thoracic region were visible. Blood started seeping from the body, and then there was this odor. At first the odor was sort of bearable but then it became more concentrated, and made me start to cough.

"Are you all right, Joyce?" they asked me.

I lied, saying, "I am fine. I am fine. I am fine, fine." Actually I felt like running out the room and never coming back.

They somewhat sensed my discomfort, and the pathologist said that if it was too much for me, I could leave. Then she mentioned the good fortune I had in seeing such a thing. There are only about four autopsies annually at the hospital and I had such luck to be there on a day when one was actually being performed. I still wanted to leave, despite my obvious luck, but I figured that it couldn't possibly take that much longer and in no time I would be out of there. The thought of appearing weak-stomached in front of a member of my aspired profession also kept me from leaving.

The lungs were removed, pieces were sliced off for analysis, and they were weighed, labeled and put in containers with liquid. I was informed that this woman was a non-smoker, for the colors of her lungs were a pale pink. To me her lungs looked sort of like Spam, with tiny, black lines running all over them.

The odor continued to get worse as the heart was cut out of the body. The pathologist explained and showed me all the parts of the heart, where the surgery was done, and when she cut open the arteries she found the cause of death: thrombus (blood clots). I started feeling some joy, for now that the cause of death had been established, there would be no need to continue, but, oh no! The pathologist had to check everything in the abdominal cavity. I was sure that maybe only an hour or so had passed, but it felt like I had been inside this windowless room for days. I wanted to look at my watch, but I was afraid of doing so, afraid of moving the latex gloves that covered my wrist. I was sure that I could have used time as a valid reason for having to leave (not that I was so sick that I wanted to puke) for I could tell the pathologist that my clinical time was over and I had another appointment — another lie.

By this time, my stomach felt so sick that I wanted to cry. I wanted to wipe this whole learning experience from my head as if it had never happened. As if I wasn't sick enough, the conversation turned to food, barbecues. Then momentary visions of human body parts grilling over charcoal floated through my head. My eyes started tearing. I was wearing protective eyewear, so I figured that they couldn't possibly see the tears that threatened to start flowing. The face of the dead woman was no longer visible. All that could be seen was the large slab of skin with yellow fat, holes in the thoracic cavity where organs had been, and, of course, blood. Oozes and oozes of it, so much blood that the pathologist frequently stopped and washed away some of it. Some of the blood was gotten rid of by sucking it up with a tube-like vacuum.

We moved along into the intestines, the kidney and the reproductive organs. As before, the pathologist explained and showed me all of it. Finally just as my stomach was about to explode, I was afraid the vomit would land on the corpse, the pathologist announced that she was finished. Incredibly, I instantly felt better. The thought of being out of this room totally reversed my symptoms of feeling sick.

I began thanking her, telling her how much I had learned about the human body, how much I would share the experience with the class, and how much I admired her for being able to do this kind of work. I removed my gloves, glanced at my watch and realized that I had been in this room for almost five hours! She said that she knew that I had wanted to run out of the room several times, especially when I had started coughing. Then she added, “Another thing that you are going need in order to be doctor is perseverance! I am sure you realize by now that perseverance pays off!”

That experience had a profound effect on me. When I got out to the parking lot, I sat for almost a half an hour before I could start the car. I sat there thinking about the fragility of life, and I was amazed at the color of human fat; such a bright yellow, almost as bright as a daisy.

I shared the experience with my E.M.T. class. I described the blood, the smell, and the shape, sizes, and color of the organs, and, like the pathologist, they repeated my luck at having seen an autopsy, which made me appreciate my organs very much.

~ ~ ~ ~ ~ ~ ~

Clinicals

I had another profound experience while I was a Certified Nursing Assistant (C.N.A) student at a community college. This class was very small and we met five times per week from 5 p.m. to 9:30 p.m. Our teacher was a woman, a retired nurse who was loved by all of her students. She was kind, honest, and, unlike many teachers, she really cared about her students. Because of her example the class took on a very relaxed air. One student baked us cookies on Fridays, another took coffee, and before long, it was like a family. One member of our class had a baby with cystic fibrosis. Of course I had no idea what it was. He explained to the class about the daily massage of the baby's lung to loosen mucus in the lungs and the fact that the baby never had a hard stool, but rather stool resembling diarrhea. The whole class felt for this parent, and just like a real family, we looked after our fellow student who was dealing with such a tremendous way of life while at the same time holding a full time job.

The course required us to be in a nursing home, wearing uniforms and name tags, etc. It was exciting to see everyone clad in white clothes and looking so professional. We were confident, well prepared and accompanying our caring teacher at very posh nursing home. We were all going to be paired with a C.N.A. and familiarize ourselves with every chore that the C.N.A. did. The duties included bathing, dressing, feeding, changing sheets, changing the diapers of incontinent patients, and making sure that their dentures were cleaned, their hair combed, and that the patient was as cared for as much as possible.

We were introduced to the staff of the nursing home and given a tour of the facility. This was one of the more expensive facilities and I think that it was about $4,000 per month to live there. The decor was nice; the painted walls had interesting wall paper borders, the dining room had tablecloths and colorful patterns on the fabric of the chairs. Each room had a television, and the carpet was clean.

I was paired with a C.N.A. who had moved to Florida from New York. She said she loved her job and was doing it, not for the money, but because she really cared about the patients. She said she should retire, but then she complained of being bored if she didn't work, so she worked part time. She told me that she calls all her patients by their proper name. No "Gramps" or "Grandma", but "Mr." "Mrs." or "Miss" as the case may be. She explained to me that being a C.N.A. involved a routine, a very carefully planned one. First there was dinner, then activities or television watching, and then you prepared the patients for bed. It didn't sound too hard.

First we proceeded to the dining room since I was going to help serve food to the patients. I was supposed to pay strict attention to the label on each person's place setting as some patients were on special diets. For example some couldn't have sugar or salt, and some could only have specially pureed food. Each patient sat in a designated spot. Those who could walk were encouraged to do so, while the patients who were wheelchair bound were wheeled to their usual place.

I smiled as I did my assigned tasks, and said hello to everyone. Then as the food was being served, the C.N.A. explained to me that the patients, who are medically able, do have a menu that they choose from.

Things were going great. I was handing out food, pouring juice, and felt so good about being able to cater to all these senior citizens. Then, just after I served some cranberry juice, I noticed a patient walking toward me. Of course, I cheerfully asked her if she needed anything but she didn't answer. I repeated my offer of assistance. Still she didn't answer, but walked right up to me. I wondered if she was all right, and then I wondered if she could speak, for some of the patients had neck surgery and couldn't speak. Her eyes were fixated on me and as soon as she reached me, she grabbed my wrist with a firm hand. I was startled, not only by her grabbing my wrist, but also the fact that for an elderly woman, she had a tight, strong grip. She grabbed my shoulder with her other hand and she stared into my eyes. That was when I noticed that her blue eyes had tears forming in them.

"I want to go home. Please take me home," she whispered.

Without realizing what I was doing, I wriggled out her grasp and ran. I ran to the elevator, through the lobby and into the parking lot. There I leaned on my car and cried. At first I couldn't understand why I was crying; I thought that I was crying because I felt sad for this woman. Sad that despite paying $4000 per month to live in such an affluent nursing home, the woman was miserable. Or maybe it was just that I was sensitive and because she had tears in her eyes, I was crying. I didn't know that a fellow student saw me running and followed me.

I was startled when I heard the familiar voice ask, "You OK, Joyce?"

I nodded my head and my classmate said, "You're not OK. You're crying," and came closer to hug me. The hug made me cry even harder, for here I was, all nicely dressed in my professional white and crying on my classmate's shoulder in a parking lot. I cried harder because my weakness was made visible without my being prepared for it.

I was handed a Kleenex and after blowing my nose, I said, "The little old lady said that I should take her home and she had tears in her eyes." I waited to see the response from my classmate and there wasn't any so I continued, "She touched something inside me. I don't know how to explain it, but when she said that, it was as if I became her for a split second." My classmate nodded.

"I felt her pain, and I felt something else, something that I can't really express."

"I think I know what you mean," said my classmate, and I looked at her sort of strange. What was it that I felt that I couldn't express in words?

"Joyce, I think what you felt was your own humanity. I think that what happened was that you became afraid you might end up like her in a nursing home, not wanting to be there. Even in such an upscale place."

I stopped crying. That was it! I looked at the old lady and I saw myself, and I must have thought of my family leaving me in such a place. Surrounded by other old, sick people. At that moment my outlook changed, for up until then as a C.N.A. I had been thinking only about the physical well-being of the patients: are they changed as soon as they need to be? Are their beds clean? Now it occurred to me that the mental environment of the patients had to be looked at, too. How would I feel if all I saw each and every day were old people? Old people in wheel chairs, blind old people, people drooling as they eat, and people who saw things, or spoke to people who weren't even real. What would be my outlook? Would I want to stay in such a place, even though the wallpaper is nice and the facility is rated like a five star hotel? No I wouldn't! My classmate was right. I wasn't crying solely because of sympathy for the old lady, I was crying because I saw my own mortality and the undeniable fact that one day, I, too, would be old and lose control of my life.

I took a deep breath and I felt better. My classmate held me by the shoulders and we headed back for the second floor. In the elevator, she spoke again.

"By the way, Joyce, the old lady who grabbed your arm has dementia, and she grabs everyone's arm and ask them to take her home."

I looked at my classmate in disbelief. Here I was with the assumption that this old lady was begging me to take her home. ME, and only me! I had felt sad, I cried and I even felt my own humanity because of her, and she says this to everybody! We laughed loudly in the elevator, for my classmate had saved the best information for last.

We walked back into the dining room and just as we entered, the same old lady was gripping the arm of another wheelchair-bound patient, in the same manner in which she had gripped mine, and the gripped patient looked uncomfortable.

My classmate and I looked at each other and I said, "I will take care of it," and walked over to the old lady. She looked up as I was approaching, let go of the wrist of the other patient and hugged me as if I were some long lost friend or family member and said, "It so nice to see you again Stephanie. How was your trip to Hawaii?"

At first I was tempted to tell her that I was not Stephanie, and that I had never been to Hawaii, but when she looked at me with such hope of news, I said, "It so nice to see you, too." I led her back to her seat and to her untouched meal.

Joyce Palmer was born in Jamaica. Her first novel, GREENWICHTOWN, is scheduled to be published soon by St.Martins Press. She lives in Florida with her husband and two children, and is currently working on her second novel.

RJDockery

Losing Rain

by Terra Pressler

Anthropologist Parker Stevens fights to keep her adopted native daughter, Rain, when the government challenges custody in retaliation for her efforts on behalf of the tribe. Parker still loves the girl's father, Night Star, who divorced Parker and their son years before and married a tribal woman. When Night Star's daughter by his tribal wife is banished, he asks Parker to raise the child. Parker's initial resistance has long since melted into deep love for Rain by the time of this hearing.

From the novel, FIRST WOMAN.

The flashing cameras frightened three-year-old Rain and she clung to Parker's skirt. A dozen voices shouted at them simultaneously.

"Prof. Stevens, are you prepared to lose your daughter?"

"I'm not going to lose my daughter."

"Do you think this hearing is a conspiracy by the government to shut you up about the Manzi?"

"What do you think?"

The courtroom was packed. Parker steered the children to a bench at the front where she could see them from counsel table.

The Children's Protective Services worker who testified first was a well-scrubbed young man with tremendous sincerity. They'd chosen well. There was a time in her life she would have admonished herself for thinking so cynically. Now she wondered at her own naiveté. Why hadn't she seen this coming?

"Mr. Jacobs, this hearing isn't about the qualities of the Stevens household, correct?" The government attorney was also well chosen. An older, maternal woman, everybody's grandma.

"No, Ma'am. As far as we know, Prof. Stevens' home is adequate for rearing children."

"So there's no need to get into allegations of negligence or lack thereof, correct?"

Parker leaned in to her attorney, "Isn't that like asking if I'm still beating my wife?"

The lawyer whispered, "If we object, we shoot ourselves in the foot by implicitly agreeing quality of care isn't at issue here."

"But if we don't and the judge doesn't let us bring it up anyway? You said we might not be allowed. The press will be left with unanswered questions about supposed negligence."

Parker's attorney reluctantly got to his feet. "Objection, Your Honor, this line of questioning is misleading and immaterial to the state's case. Prof. Stevens is an exceptional mother, as we intend to show."

"Sustained. And, no, you will not show. The defendant's parenting is not at issue here. I would caution both counsel from trying their cases to the press. We all know the law here. What say we stick to it and avoid grandstanding?"

Parker's attorney made no cross-examination. Parker turned on him, amazed. "Aren't you at least going to ask how long these cases normally take? Why this one is being brought so quickly on the heels of my son's public support of the Manzi? How are we going to establish conspiracy?"

"Conspiracy to defraud civil rights is a separate counterclaim and will be tried in the final hearing in Federal Court, not here. This is only to determine temporary custody."

"I can't believe this." Parker felt her face go pale. If Rain were forced to live with complete strangers after everything she'd endured. . .

The government's next witness was John TwoFeather, a tall, stocky man. Parker turned to her attorney, "He's a Plains Indian, what's he doing here?"

"Mr. TwoFeather, will you tell the court your occupation, please."

"I represent the Council of Elders of the Nation of Confederated Tribes."

"And does the area covered in the Nation of Confederated Tribes include the Squanomie River tribes?"

"Yes, it does."

"And has the Council, at the government's request, selected a family capable of rearing an Indian child?"

"We have."

"Now, Mr. TwoFeather, I'm going to anticipate what I'm guessing the defendant will object to and ask you straight out: the tribes in the Squanomie River basin are different than the Plains tribes, are they not?"

"Every tribe is different from every other tribe."

"Yes, of course, but the river basin tribes are especially different in that they've had very little contact, traditionally, with plains tribes or whites generally, is that correct?"

"Yes."

"And what, if anything, has the Council done in its selection to take that fact into account?"

"We have chosen a family from the river tribes. They

live here in the city."

"So, Rain would keep her river basin culture, correct?"

"Yes."

"And she could still see her brother?"

"Yes. The family has said they will allow visits with the brother."

Parker felt her throat close. She turned to find Bright Star. He sat with Rain, his face agonized. It was a mistake to bring them here.

"Mr. TwoFeather, is the family chosen for Rain here in court today?"

"Yes."

"Could you point them out, please?"

The strong old man pointed toward the back.

The judge interjected, "Will the proposed family please stand?"

From the back of the courtroom a well-dressed, small-statured man and woman rose. Even from this distance Parker could tell their tribe.

Bright Star was on his feet, his voice loud and outraged. "They are Co'oru, enemies of the Manzi. You cannot take my sister away and put her with these people. She is my sister and we belong together. We are Manzi!"

The judge's gavel cracked, as the court erupted at Bright Star's outburst. "Young man, this is a court of law. You will act with appropriate decorum or be ushered out."

Bright Star sat, but held Rain as if he would physically fight anyone who tried to take her away. Rain clung to Bright Star's neck, eyes wide.

When the judge called an hour's recess for lunch, Parker dropped her face into her hands. She didn't care how defeated she must look to the press, to her children. Her children. She sat up and swiveled in her seat. They sat like boards, side by side, staring at her. She went to them and squeezed in between, each of them curled into the crook of one of her arms. The press was off hounding the native elder and the Co'oru couple. The new darlings. What an ironic, boomerang punishment for their efforts to increase native awareness. It was almost too Machiavellian in its perfect revenge.

She held her children, banishing the corroding thought this could be the last time they were together. Prof. Tuis dropped behind her and put his gnarled old hands on her shoulders. "It's not over, yet."

No, there'd be more hell to pay, and then it would be over.

True to his word, the judge wouldn't allow evidence about Parker's parenting abilities or Rain's adaptation to their home. Parker was able to outline the basic facts of how Rain came to be with them and that was all. Then she faced cross-examination.

"Ms. Stevens . . . " The government attorney steadfastly refused to use Parker's academic title, a classic tactic to diminish credibility.

"Ms. Stevens, you have no Native American blood, correct?"

"Not to my knowledge."

"None whatsoever?"

"Not as far as I know."

The government attorney smiled a brief, cold smile. "You have never been registered with any tribe, nor have your parents or grandparents been so registered, correct?"

"Yes."

"There is nothing remotely indigenous in your background that would . . ."

"Your Honor, counsel's made the point." Parker had

begun to wonder if her attorney had any fight in him. He had at least this much.

"Just wanted to nail down the state's case, Your Honor."

"You've sufficiently addressed this point, Counsel. Proceed."

"Ms. Stevens, you claimed in your direct Rain's father appointed you her guardian, isn't that true?"

"Well, more or le . . "

"'Yes' or 'no' will suffice, Ms. Stevens."

"Yes."

"But you have nothing in writing to that effect?"

"No, but . . . "

"Thank you Ms. Stevens, you answered my question."

"Now, isn't it true you used to be married to Rain's father, at least 'married' in the Manzi way?"

"Yes."

"And it was during this time you conceived Bright Star?"

"Yes."

"And isn't it true when Bright Star was six years old, your 'mate' Night Star abruptly divorced you?"

"What was that, Ms. Stevens? I'm having trouble hearing you."

Parker's voice came out a rasp. "Yes."

"And didn't that divorce involve a brutal, humiliating ceremony in which the entire tribe symbolically struck you, driving you from their lives forever?"

Where was she getting this? Bright Star would never have told anyone . . .

"I don't know if you could call it brutal . . ."

"Answer the question, Ms. Stevens. Was the divorce procedure humiliating?"

Parker stared at the polished oak railing on the witness stand. Her voice was barely a whisper. "Yes."

"Yes. And your former mate was well-aware, was he not, what the divorce ceremony would entail?"

"Objection, Your Honor, of what possible relevance..."

The government lawyer interrupted, "I have a specific place I'm heading, Your Honor. With the court's indulgence?"

"You'd better, Counsel. Proceed."

"Now, Ms. Stevens, after the divorce, you didn't see your former husband for ten years, is that correct?"

"Yes."

"No communication whatsoever."

"No."

"No child support, no visitation?"

"Under Manzi law . . ."

"Ms. Stevens, I remind you to just answer the question."

"I'm trying to . . . "

"Ms. Stevens, during those ten years did your former husband have any contact whatsoever with you?"

"No, but . . ."

"I see. Yet you are trying to tell this court that after an acrimonious divorce and ten years without any contact whatsoever, your former husband shows up one day and miraculously grants you custody of his beloved child by his new wife. Is that right?"

"Well, it's not like you make it sound."

"Why, Ms. Stevens, that's exactly what you've testified here today. Your husband divorces you in a vicious manner, ignores you and your son for ten years, then magically turns up just when needed to tell you he chooses you to rear his daughter by another woman.

"I explained why Rain was here and why she couldn't return to her ho . . ."

"Thank you, Ms. Stevens, I think you've explained more than enough. Redirect."

"No questions, your Honor. The defense calls Prof. Albert Tuis."

"Prof. Tuis, we've established you're the world's leading authority on the Manzi. Will you tell me, sir, do the Manzi have a written language?" Parker's attorney was leaning toward the witness box as if willing his answers.

Prof. Tuis adjusted his glasses and cleared his throat. "No. Certain objects are identified by symbols, but their history, law and culture are communicated through a series of teaching stories handed down orally."

"I see. Then would there be any way Night Star would be able to write?"

"No. Of course not."

"So, presumably then, it would be impossible for Night Star to provide any written document to Prof. Stevens regarding his wishes concerning his daughter."

"Correct."

"Prof. Tuis, what if any knowledge do you have concerning Prof. Stevens' assertion that Night Star granted her informal guardianship of Rain?"

"I was there on the evening Night Star said he wanted Prof. Stevens to be Rain's "other mother", the Manzi way of saying surrogate mother, or guardian."

"And why would a man who has divorced his wife ask her to rear his child by another woman?"

The state's attorney flew to her feet. "Objection, calls for a conclusion . . ."

"Your Honor, we have established Prof. Tuis as an expert on Manzi culture. Who better to tell us whether behavior which may appear odd to us isn't perfectly compatible with Manzi codes of conduct?"

"Overruled. Proceed."

"Prof. Tuis, answer the question please: why would a Manzi who had divorced his wife ask her to rear his child by a new wife?"

Prof. Tuis paused, cleared his throat and looked at Parker as if to apologize for what was only the truth. "It is my belief Night Star continues to love Prof. Stevens and trusts her above all others."

It hadn't been the answer Parker's attorney expected and he wrapped up his direct without further questions. The government attorney treated Prof. Tuis with great deference on cross-examination, aware of his reputation and community standing.

"Prof. Tuis, you're an expert on the Manzi; isn't it true it's a matrilineal culture?"

"That's correct."

"Indeed, I know that from your excellent treatise on the Manzi. And Prof. Tuis, being a matrilineal culture, what the woman says about her children goes, correct?"

"Yes."

"Which is to say, under Manzi law the mother has paramount rights regarding children and the father has no say one way or another, correct?"

"Well, I wouldn't say 'no say' at all . . . "

"And Night Star continues to be married to Blue Sky, correct?"

"Yes."

"Now, if a child is banished by the mother, that's it, right? That's not something the father can overrule, isn't that true?"

Prof. Tuis cleared his throat. "Normally, yes. That would be the case."

"So, under Manzi law, Night Star had no right to award

the care of his child to Ms. Stevens or anyone else, since Rain's mother had banished her, isn't that right?"

"Well, yes, under Manzi law; however this court . . ."

"Thank you, Prof. Tuis, that will be all."

Prof. Tuis ignored the government attorney and spoke directly to the judge. "Your Honor, wouldn't the law of this court apply viz. a viz. Night Star's legal authority over his child?"

"Objection, Your Honor, nonresponsive. Please instruct the witness he's to refrain from extemporizing . . . "

"Relax, Counsel. All this can be argued later. But frankly, Prof. Tuis' point is well-taken."

The government attorney's face briefly lost the grandmotherly warmth she'd so carefully cultivated. "No further questions."

The judge mumbled "Redirect" and Parker's attorney jumped to attention. "Prof. Tuis, Night Star's intention regarding his child has been brought up. Why isn't he here to testify?"

"Night Star lives a day by truck and two days by dugout canoe down the Squanomie River from here. Prof. Stevens was served with notice of this hearing two days ago. It was impossible to notify him in time."

"No further questions."

The government attorney got to her feet. "Your Honor, I have just one rebuttal witness. The State calls Dustin Prootum to the stand."

Dusty. That's where the government attorney got all her information. Parker cursed the day she ever saw him, cursed herself for trusting him enough to tell him about her life.

"Dr. Prootum, during your relationship with Ms. Stevens, were you ever privy to her interest in the Manzi?"

"Yes. I'm an archival librarian, so besides knowing Ms.

Stevens personally, I also saw her professionally."

"Do you remember anything happening in that professional capacity?"

"Ms. Stevens asked me to pull every article in our microfiche that mentioned the Manzi."

"And did you?"

"Certainly. That's my job."

"What happened after that?"

"Profes . . . Ms. Stevens came back to my desk in a very agitated state and demanded I make notarized copies of several of the articles."

"Is such a request unusual?"

"Yes, it is, especially in the urgent manner she made it."

"Did she tell you why she wanted the copies?"

"She said she'd discovered evidence that government actions taken to save the Squanomie Resort Community thirty years ago had accidentally caused some Manzi to drown."

"And what was her reaction to this information?"

"She was like an insane person seeking vengeance. Like it was some monstrous crime instead of a tragic accident that happened decades ago."

"And what was your response?"

"I tried to calm her down. We were friends, close friends at the time. At least I thought we were."

"What was her response to your efforts to calm her?"

"She was insufferably rude, terminated our friendship on the spot and stomped away."

"I object, Your Honor, what possible relevance . . . ?"

"The next questions will answer that, Your Honor."

"Proceed."

"Dr. Prootum, has Ms. Stevens benefited personally from her involvement with the Manzis?"

"Certainly. Her academic reputation is based upon her

Manzi research."

"I see. Now, Dr. Prootum, based on your personal and professional knowledge of Ms. Stevens, do you believe in her efforts to champion the Manzi and go after the government she is capable of lying, specifically of lying about her supposed relationship to the child Rain?"

Dusty looked directly at Parker. "Absolutely."

Closing arguments were surprisingly brief. The government attorney hammered the clear language of the Uniform Indian Adoption Act. The facts were simple and uncompromising: Rain was a full-blooded native whose family had abandoned her.

Parker Stevens had no Indian blood. A native family had been found that met the requirements of the act. There was nothing more to say.

On the contrary, Parker's attorney claimed, Rain's father had not abandoned her and had rather awarded guardianship to Prof. Stevens, who not only had exceptional knowledge of Manzi culture, but whose son was Rain's beloved half-brother. It clearly would not be in the best interests of this child to tear her from her true family.

The government counsel had the last word and reminded the judge that the usual best interests of the child standard did not apply in this case. Under the clear language of the act, the best interests of the child were per se met by placing her with a native family. Any supposed guardianship was based on hearsay and, in Ms. Stevens case, highly suspect hearsay.

Before the judge even started speaking, the sorrowful compassion in his look told Parker she'd lost. She surely understood the difficult position the court was in . . . the law was clear . . . if further evidence arose, it could be presented at the final hearing.

Parker heard the gavel and felt the room spinning out of control. She saw a woman Sheriff's Deputy bear down on Rain from the back of the room.

"Wait, please, let me get her." Parker rushed from her seat.

"Mom, no." Bright Star was crying. He held Rain like a drowning man holding the last bit of raft between himself and a raging sea.

Parker felt emptied, disembodied. Mechanically, she caressed Bright Star's head as she took Rain from him. His arms fell away reluctantly, disbelieving. Parker put her face into Rain's hair. There was nothing so sweet as freshly washed baby hair. Would the Co'oru wash her hair gently, folding a wash cloth around her forehead to avoid getting soap in her eyes? Even the baby shampoo stung if it got in her eyes. She needed to tell them how Rain liked her hair washed.

The deputy took Rain out of her arms. Parker instinctively reached for her child as Rain let out a flat, eerie howl and struggled with all her three-year-old fury to return to her new mother. But she was being carried away.

Parker watched through dazed eyes as Rain and the deputy made their way down the aisle to the Co'oru couple, a blitz of flashing cameras adding to Rain's panic.

Suddenly, the media pack turned away from Rain and ran toward the door.

It was Night Star. He was in Manzi winter dress, breechcloth over leggings, a red shirt encircled by a cougar claw necklace.

When Rain caught sight of her father, she struggled

against the deputy, but the woman held tight. Rain gave a fierce cry, then bit the woman's arm. Startled, the deputy dropped her and Rain flung herself into her father's arms, laughing and sobbing. Night Star put his arm around Rain, as if daring anyone to challenge his absolute right to do so. The press and gallery, erupting in pandemonium a moment before, just as suddenly fell hushed. From the corner of her eye, Parker saw the bailiff rush into the judge's chambers.

Out of the uneasy silence, the state's attorney ordered the deputy to proceed with transferring custody. The deputy stayed glued to the floor and stared at Night Star, despite the attorney's increasingly shrill commands.

From behind her, Parker heard the bailiff. "All rise. This court is now in session."

The attorneys flew back to counsel tables as the judge took the three steps to his place behind the bench.

"Counsel, it is my understanding a significant witness has appeared."

Parker's attorney rushed to speak first. "That's correct, Your Honor. The defense would call Night Star."

The government attorney was on her feet. "Objection, Your Honor. This hearing is over and a ruling has been made. If counsel for the defense wishes to call another witness, he should do so at the final hearing."

The judge shook his finger at the government's attorney. "Counsel, a little girl's well-being is at stake here. I'm not inclined to let procedural niceties get in the way. Considering the rush with which the state brought this case, it's amazing Mr. Star is here at all." The judge nodded at Parker's attorney. "You may proceed."

Prof. Tuis translated. He told the judge the Manzi were

virtually incapable of lying, given their strong belief that to do so would impinge on a good death, but Night Star was nonetheless required to swear an oath. He swore by First Woman to speak from his heart.

"Mr. Star, are you the father of the child known as Rain Star, the child sitting on that bench?"

"He says he is."

"And have you abandoned your child?"

There was extended dialogue between Night Star and Prof. Tuis.

"Your Honor, Night Star says despite the decision of Rain's mother to divorce Rain from the tribe, he continues to be her father. He is a man sworn to honor his children."

"Now, Mr. Star, when you realized Rain could not return to the tribe, what did you do?"

"He says he came to the Empty One city to appoint Parker guardian, literally 'other mother', to his daughter."

"And is it your intention that your daughter be raised by Parker Stevens?"

"He says it is."

"Will you continue to be involved in your daughter's life?"

"He says he will be."

"I have no further questions, Your Honor."

"The state may cross-examine."

"Thank you, Your Honor. Mr. Star, you mentioned the words "Empty One". To what does that refer?"

"He says you are Empty Ones. Empty Ones are whites."

"I see. And isn't that why your wife divorced Rain from the tribe, because she'd been contaminated by Empty Ones?"

"He says, 'yes'."

"So, to a Manzi, Empty Ones are evil. Bad people, isn't that correct?"

"He says this is so."

"Well, Mr. Star, if Empty Ones are evil, why in the world would you want your supposedly cherished daughter raised among them?"

"Night Star says he used to believe all Empty Ones were evil, but since meeting Honored Tuis and Parker, he knows this is not so, that some Empty Ones are good and honorable people."

"But wouldn't it in fact be better for Rain to be raised by indigenous people?"

"He says he doesn't want his daughter to be raised by strangers, whether they're indigenous people or not; he wants his daughter to be raised by Parker."

With a frustrated little sniff, the government attorney took another tack. "Mr. Star, you claim to be Rain's father. Do you have any proof of that?"

"Your Honor, I don't know how to translate this. The Manzi have no word for "proof." Let me do this: I'll ask Night Star if there is any way to show the truth that he is Rain's father."

When Prof. Tuis translated the question, Night Star's face balled in consternation. Finally he spoke.

"He says he does not understand this. Who else could he be?"

"Who else, indeed?" The attorney for the state arched her eyebrows in high skepticism. "It strikes me as amazingly opportune that a man who lives three days away - by dugout canoe, no less - shows up at the eleventh hour just in time to reclaim his daughter."

"Counsel, is there a question in all that or are you making your closing early?"

"Pardon me, Your Honor. Mr. Star, or whoever you are, would you be willing to submit to a blood test to establish whether or not you're Rain's biological father?"

Tuis translated. In a single, fluid movement, Night Star leapt to his feet, drew his knife and slashed a deep cut in his hand. He held his bleeding palm out to the government attorney, the bright red blood dripping silently onto the grey courtroom floor.

With a tiny gasp, counsel for the state shrank back in her chair. "I . . . the state will stipulate paternity."

The judge's ruling was brief. "The state has failed to prove its case. Dismissed."

Terra Pressler is an award-winning playwright who has written professionally since 1986. She has placed nonfiction in publications as diverse as Sports Illustrated and Yoga Journal. She teaches creative writing and co-ordinates Lifelong Writers at the University of South Florida Lifelong Learning department in Tampa.

Children's Stories

Children's Story

The Hidden Star

by Claudia Sodaro

There was, once upon a time, a six-year-old boy named Gary.

"Daddy's working on the computer, Mommy is feeding the dog and the dog is busy eating," he recited to his stuffed bear. Thank goodness Grammy was visiting his home that very weekend. She always had splendid ideas and he was forever curious.

Grammy realized that there was a whole world on the farm which Gary had not yet explored. She suggested that Gary go on a real-life journey nearby. "Search for something that is red, round and beautiful that has a star inside it," she encouraged.

Grammy loved the fresh smell of the outdoors and being surrounded by the lush green, growth. She offered to go along on Gary's journey. He welcomed the company of his Grammy, who was still very limber and able to take long walks every day.

Since this was Gary's journey, Grammy reminded Gary that he could ask any questions along the way that might help him to find the red, round, beautiful object that had a star inside it. He and Grammy headed down the path which led from the boy's house to the open farmlands. Gary met a merry little girl humming a tune in the sunshine. Her cheeks were like pink blossom petals. She was singing like a cardinal.

"Do you know where I shall find a red, round object that has a star inside it?" Gary asked her.

"Ask my father," said the little girl. "He is a farmer and knows these lands better than anyone in the area. Perhaps he will know."

Gary understood that the questions and the journey were all going to be of his own doing. He noticed that his Grammy was right along beside him.

The young explorer approached the farmer who was moving barrels of large potatoes, baskets of yellow squash and golden pumpkins. He looked around at all the harvested vegetables and wondered if perhaps the object would somehow be in this farmer's great, brown barn.

"Do you know where I shall find a red, round object that has a star inside it?" Gary asked the farmer.

The farmer, who knew the lands in this area better than anyone, thought for a minute and remarked that the only stars he ever gazed upon were up in the sky. They were not surrounded by red, round objects.

"However," said the farmer. "My own granny lives at

the foot of the hill, and she knows how to make molasses, taffy, popcorn balls and red mittens. Perhaps she can direct you better than I can."

Gary went farther still, until he came to the farmer's granny who was sitting in her pretty garden of herbs and marigolds. She was as wrinkled as a walnut and as warm and pleasant as the sunshine.

"Please dear Granny," said the eager Gary, wanting to find a red, round object that had a star inside it. "Could you help me find something special that I am looking for?"

The Granny was knitting a red mitten. When she heard the little boy's question, she laughed so hard that the ball of woolen yarn rolled out of her lap and down to the little path paved with pebbles.

"I would like to find that object myself," she confided. "It would be nice to own an object that had a star inside it. I could look at it during the daytime. It would shine even when the stars are not able to be seen because of the brightness of the great, yellow sun."

"But," said the Granny in all her wisdom, "ask the wind which blows about wherever it wishes and listens at all the chimney tops. Perhaps the wind can direct you better."

Gary thanked the wise woman and went on up the hill getting farther and farther from his own farm. It was beginning to get cooler. Evening was setting in and he was extremely glad to have his own Grammy right beside him.

The wind was coming down the hill as Gary attempted to climb it. As they met, the wind turned about and went along, singing beside Gary. It whistled in his ear and pushed him. The wind dropped a pretty leaf into his hands.

"Oh wind," asked a tired but determined Gary. "We have gone along together quite a while. Can you help me to find a red, round object that has a star inside it?"

The wind, not able to speak in words that we understand, went singing ahead of Gary until it brought him back to his own farm and into the orchard.

There in the orchard, the wind climbed higher and with its powerful force shook the branches of an apple tree. There at his feet, lay a large, shiny apple.

Gary picked up the apple. It was as much as his two hands could hold. The apple was as red as the sun had been able to paint it. The thick brown stem stood up as straight as a chimney.

At last Grammy spoke to Gary because the wind could not convey its message any further. Grammy instructed Gary to bring the apple inside. Gary asked one last time, "Grammy, have I found the red, round object that has a star inside it?"

Grammy gently took the plump, red apple from her grandson and carefully cut it across the thickest, fleshiest part of the fruit. Smiling with delight, Gary gazed upon a beautiful star inside the apple. The star was created by the seeds and the core of the apple. How amazing it was!

Gary realized at that point that not only did he love to eat apples, especially with his Grammy, but that he always looked for the hidden star inside.

To this day round, red objects that have stars inside them grow on Gary's very own farm. Like his Grammy, he continues to take part in nature's journey to discover how special and beautiful this world really is.

Claudia Sodaro's experience as educator, playground director, grandmother and babysitter, account for the ample ideas in her stories. The eldest of four siblings and more than eighty cousins, she has been afforded the rich opportunity always to be surrounded by children.

Kosher Kat

by Janice Perelman

The cat dragged herself out of the thick icy undergrowth. She slowly walked closer to the large building. A patch of golden light fell onto the black ground through frosted windows, momentarily catching her in its glow. Her orange and gray fur was matted and dirty. Were people nearby? Was it safe here? Suddenly bright lights rounded the corner, and cars began to park, bringing people to a meeting at the temple. Each time the wide temple doors opened, the light inside beckoned to the cat to enter.

"Perhaps there will be a bowl of milk inside, or a dish

of food, or a warm corner just right for me to curl up and sleep in," the cat thought. As the last two people went inside, she dashed between their legs and entered the foyer. How nice and warm it felt inside. Without warning, she was caught by strong hands. All the squirming in the world could not set her free.

"Look at that dirty cat! Get it out of here at once!" cried a woman.

"I've got it," answered the man beside her, and the cat once again found herself outside in the blustery darkness. She felt her belly complain about its emptiness, a reminder of her lack of food, as if she needed one.

The cat crouched under a nearby shrub and waited. Finally, people began to leave the temple. Just as the last couple left, the cat dashed inside the doorway, her striped tail just missing the door's closing. Her strong sense of smell led her to the temple's kitchen where she hastily gobbled the tuna from leftover sandwiches. With her paw, she overturned the small creamer of milk which she drained dry, just the thing to quench her thirst. Now satisfied, she began to explore the temple in the dim light. She went no farther than the boiler room. There she curled up in a corner and went to sleep for the night, warm and content for the first time in a long while.

For several weeks, she continued to sleep in the boiler room and to live on leftovers or garbage in the kitchen. Fred, the custodian, opened the outside door near the boiler room several times a day, so she was able to run out and return unseen. Until one morning.

"Well, what do we have here?" asked Fred. "Who invited you in?"

The cat ran back to her safe corner in the boiler room and stared at him with unblinking green eyes, only the tip of her tail moving slightly.

"This here is no hotel, cat. You'll just have to find somewhere else to live." Fred picked her up, carried her down the hall, and placed her firmly but gently outside. "Now, scat!"

Before she could make a move, the door was closed behind her.

Now what could she do? The cold March winds had picked up, whirling circles of dry, flaking leaves into the air around her. Children began arriving for Hebrew classes.

"Maybe one of them will pick me up," she thought. "Maybe they'll take me back inside, or to their house." Maybe. She meowed sadly at the arriving children. Although they noticed her and some even called "Hi, kitty," no one picked her up or let her into the temple. After a while, she even stopped meowing. Then Mark and Amy, the Rabbi's children, arrived. Unlike the others, the dark-haired girl of ten and her younger brother stopped and petted her. Mark even lifted her into his arms and held her.

"She sure looks sad and pitiful, doesn't she, Amy?"

"Yes," Amy answered, "but you'd better be careful. She might be wild. She could have a disease and make you sick."

"Let's show her to Daddy. Maybe he'll let us take her home!" Mark ventured, trying to ignore his sister's sensible warnings. Excited at the idea of having her as his pet, Mark carried her into his father's study.

"Daddy, look what we found! She doesn't even have a home. Can we keep her?" Mark asked.

Just then, Fred appeared at the Rabbi's door. "Is she still around? That's the same cat I found in the boiler room and set outside. She's probably the reason for the garbage being chewed up the last few weeks."

"Do you know if she belongs to anyone?" asked the Rabbi.

"I doubt it," Fred answered.

"Then we can take her home with us!" Mark stubbornly insisted.

The Rabbi looked over his reading glasses at Mark. "You know we can't do that, Mark. Your mother has allergies; we can't keep a pet at home."

"Can't we please keep her in the temple, Daddy?" Amy used her most persuasive tone.

"First," said the Rabbi, "we don't even know if she has an owner. Secondly, who would take care of her here? And lastly, she doesn't look too healthy."

"Oh, Daddy, we could take care of her ourselves," said Amy. "Mark and I could feed her and get a litter box for her. We're here almost every day anyway."

"I'll tell you what I will do," their father answered. "Keep the cat here while I advertise to see if she has an owner. We'll take her to the vet for an exam. And if no one claims her, then you can keep her here."

Mark and Amy jumped up and down with excitement and a sense of victory.

"Thanks, Daddy, thank you, thank you," they both yelled.

"Shhh!," said the Rabbi, "remember you're in the temple. Now go take care of the cat and let me finish my work."

"She needs a name," said Amy.

"Tom?" asked Mark.

"Patty!" suggested Amy. "We don't even know if 'she' is a girl or a boy. Until the vet can tell us, let's just call her 'Kosher Kat'. After all, she has been eating out of the temple kitchen, right?"

Kosher Kat may not have understood much about the conversation, but she could sense it was about her, and that no one was throwing her out. Her eyes narrowed as she purred with relief and contentment.

No one answered the advertisement in the newspaper.

The vet said that with a good diet and plenty of love, Kosher Kat would be fine.

"But there's something you need to know," he added. "Kosher Kat is going to be a mother soon." Naturally, Mark and Amy were delighted with this, and naturally their father was not.

Amy and Mark were so excited about Kosher Kat having kittens that they left the temple that night forgetting their next day's homework and schoolbooks in the Rabbi's study. It was after dinner by the time the children missed their books. On the short ride back to the temple to get them, the children chatted about what they would name the expected kittens. When they entered through the school door, they heard loud, excited meows coming from the boiler room.

"Something's the matter with Kosher Kat," the Rabbi said.

As he opened the door to the boiler room, Kosher Kat dashed out of the door and scooted down the hallway, where she wailed loudly.

"What's the matter with her, Daddy?" asked Mark

"I don't know," the Rabbi answered, puzzled.

Kosher Kat stopped at a storage closet, still meowing.

Following closely on Kosher Kat's heels, the Rabbi opened the closet door, and billows of smoke escaped into the hall.

"It's a fire! You children get out as fast as you can. I'll pull the alarm."

He hurried the children, who held firmly onto Kosher Kat, outside, and re-entered the building. Within minutes, the children heard sirens approaching and knew help was on the way. The Rabbi reappeared from the temple, this time grasping the Torah he had saved from the Holy Ark.

The fire was extinguished and the excitement was over

within a few minutes. Most of the damage had been confined to the closet and basement.

"Daddy, do you realize we have Kosher Kat to thank for saving the temple?" asked Amy. "If we hadn't come back for our homework and heard her meowing, it could have been a disaster!"

"Kosher Kat certainly did us a big favor, didn't she?" he responded. "And maybe her kittens will bring good luck to the families who adopt them!"

Even Fred was impressed by Kosher Kat's fire-finding ability. "You think I can have one of her kittens for my grandkids?" he asked.

"Sure, you can have first choice," Mark offered.

There was no problem in finding the kittens homes. Kosher Kat became a proud mother and was allowed to roam through all the school rooms. She was the heroine of the temple and had become a beautiful cat all the children wanted to pet. And when her kittens were old enough to be adopted, she was not lonely. She had the company of all the children, especially of Mark and Amy, and she had the memory of her wonderful adventure.

Janice Perelman holds a B.A. in English and psychology and an M.A. in Counseling/Education from U.R.I. She taught English to secondary school students, high school equivalency to adults, and Sunday school to fourth-ninth graders in Rhode Island. Janice retired from social work as Protective Services supervisor after 25 years of service to abused and neglected children in Rhode Island and Florida. She enjoys traveling, china painting, writing and reading to her five young grandchildren.

Children's Story

Teapot Trouble

by Robyn Hillary

R
00
Mad
Maria,
Mad
Jack.

Mom said, "Dirty
dishes won't attack.
Wash them all
before I'm back."

Good dishes, bad dishes,
more than five.
A greasy gooey stack
very much alive.
Sad
Maria,
Sad
Jack.

Teapot Trouble

Wrestler Teapot whistled,
"This is a blast.
I go first and
you go last."
Fast Teapot, Sneaky Teapot.

Teapot Trouble

The dishes rattled,
"That's not fair!"
Wrestler Teapot hissed,
"I don't care!"

Teapot Trouble

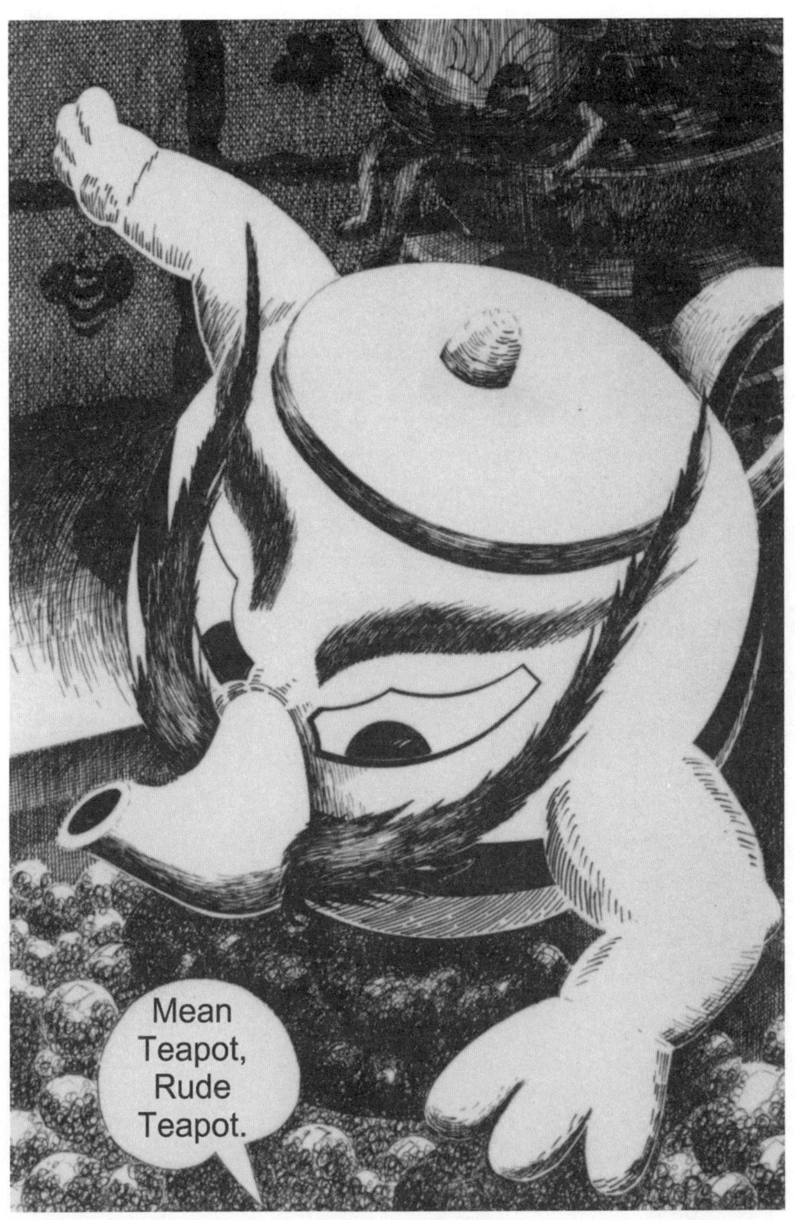

To be continued....

Robyn Hillary has a background in residential and commercial design and is pursuing her artistic career in drawing, writing and metal sculpture. Her awards include: Gasparilla 2000, Emerging Artists Program; a collection of tables for a gallery in Zurich, Switzerland, 1998/1999; drawings published in The Best of Colored Pencil 2; and multiple awards at the Dunedin Fine Art Center show, including Best of Show in pencil and metal.